CAST OF C

Emily Bryce. Owner of the Lenter̶ can do just about anything with a p̶ ̶ ̶ ̶ ̶ ̶ ̶ ̶ ̶ ̶ ̶ ̶ ̶ ̶ ̶ ̶ ̶ ̶ unusual way.

Henry Bryce. Her bemused husband, who knows to keep Emily out of the kitchen and tries to keep her out of trouble.

Lincoln "Link" Simpson. Their best friend, who owns the gun and antiques shop underneath their cluttered studio.

Mrs. Camille Lorenz. A decorator referred to admiringly by her colleagues as one of the three bitches of Fifty-Seventh Street.

Fred Wheeler. Camille's amiable husband.

Agnes Ash. Camille's devoted secretary, a pale-eyed drone of a woman.

Julian Pointer. Camille's assistant.

Pierre Marie Cloche. The United Nations ambassador from Gaad.

Francine Cloche. His pretty, luxury-loving wife.

Louis and Marie Mancini. Friends of the Bryces.

Claude Bernard. Another decorator, known to hate Camille Lorenz.

Hazen Armstrong. A developer.

Geraldine Seabrook. His bossy assistant.

August Boomer. A bill collector.

Detective Burgreen. A friendly policeman.

Plus assorted shopkeepers, friends, relatives, reporters, business associates, delivery people, and cops.

Books by Margaret Scherf

Featuring Emily and Henry Bryce
The Gun in Daniel Webster's Bust (1949)
The Green Plaid Pants (1951)
Glass on the Stairs (1954)
The Diplomat and the Gold Piano (1963)

Featuring the Reverend Martin Buell
Always Murder a Friend (1948)
Gilbert's Last Toothache (1949)
The Curious Custard Pie (1950)
The Elk and the Evidence (1952)
The Cautious Overshoes (1956)
Never Turn Your Back (1959)
The Corpse in the Flannel Nightgown (1965)

Featuring Grace Severance
The Banker's Bones (1968)
The Beautiful Birthday Cake (1971)
To Cache a Millionaire (1972)
The Beaded Banana (1978)

Featuring Lieutenant Ryan
The Owl in the Cellar (1945)
Murder Makes Me Nervous (1948)

Nonseries
The Corpse Grows a Beard (1940)
The Case of the Kippered Corpse (1941)
They Came to Kill (1942)
Dead: Senate Office Building (1953)
Judicial Body (1957)
If You Want Murder Well Done (1974)
Don't Wake Me Up While I'm Driving (1977)

For Children
The Mystery of the Velvet Box (1963)
The Mystery of the Empty Trunk (1964)
The Mystery of the Shaky Staircase (1965)

Historical Novel
Wedding Train (1960)

The Diplomat
and the Gold Piano

by Margaret Scherf

Rue Morgue Press
Lyons / Boulder

The Rue Morgue Press
P.O. Box 4119
Boulder, Colorado 80306
800-699-6214
www.ruemorguepress.com

Printed by
Johnson Printing

PRINTED IN THE UNITED STATES OF AMERICA

The Diplomat
and the Gold Piano

About Margaret Scherf

Margaret Scherf was born on April Fools' Day 1908 in Fairmont, West Virginia. Her father was a high school teacher and the family moved first to New Jersey and then to Wyoming before finally settling in Montana. After graduation from high school in Cascade, Montana, she attended Antioch College (1925-1928) in Yellow Springs, Ohio, a very small town near Dayton. She left college short of graduation to take a job as an editorial secretary with Robert M. McBride, a book publishing firm located in New York City. Wanderlust struck her in 1929 and she embarked on a round-the-world trip, an experience that would instill in her a love of travel that would stay with her for the rest of her life. Upon her return to the United States, she joined the staff of the Camp Fire Girls national magazine in 1932 (an experience she would put to use in 1948's *Murder Makes Me Nervous*), then moved on to the staff of the Wise Book Company as a secretary and copywriter in 1934. In 1939, she quit her job and launched her career as a full-time writer, publishing three mysteries with Putnam between 1940 and 1942. With the advent of World War II, she temporarily abandoned her writing career and took a job as secretary to the Naval Inspector, Bethehem Steel Shipyard in Brooklyn.

After the war, she returned to writing and eventually found herself back in Montana, a state she was to call home for the rest of her life. She continued to revisit New York settings in her books during this period, most notably in the Emily and Henry Bryce series, but her postwar books were primarily set in more rustic locales. "Small town characters, especially Episcopalians, were my delight," she wrote to a critic in 1979.

Chief among those characters was the Reverend Martin Buell, an Episcopalian minister just on the wrong side of middle age who brings both his housekeeper and a "we'll do things my way" attitude to a small Montana parish. Martin's bishop explained that things had been "slipping" in the parish and the parishioners needed a bit of "bullying." He sent the right man. Buell was to ride roughshod over his parishioners during the course of seven books published between 1948 and 1965.

Scherf alternated the Buell books with a daffy series featuring Emily and Henry Bryce, two Manhattan decorators. When we first meet them in 1949's *The Gun in Daniel Webster's Bust*, Emily is pushing Henry to marry him, an idea that doesn't sit too well with him given the fact his last marriage ended when his wife threw a cup of hot coffee in his face. But marry they did, and continued to solve crimes in their own fashion, Emily providing the right-brained, intuitive approach to crime solving while the left-brained Henry relied—more or less—on logic. The Bryce series ended in 1963 after four books.

Her other major series featured Dr. Grace Severance, a retired pathologist. This series, like Scherf herself, moved between Montana and Arizona, beginning with Arizona-based *The Banker's Bones* in 1968 and ending four books later in 1978 with *The Beaded Banana,* set in Montana. The Arizona locale was a familiar one by this time, as Scherf was now spending her winters in Quartzsite, Arizona, a small mining town near the California border, halfway between Phoenix and Las Vegas, Nevada

But she was no longer alone. In 1965, at the age of 57, she surprised friends and relatives by marrying Perry E. Beebe. She helped her husband run a cherry orchard near Yellow Bay, Montana, when she wasn't writing or tending to one of the three antique shops she owned at various times in and around Kalispell. The same year she married Perry the politically outspoken Scherf was also elected as a Democrat to the Montana state legislature. Perry died in 1975 and Peggy moved into a house she had built in Bigfork. On May 12, 1979, she was struck and killed by a drunk driver south of Kalispell.

For more information on Scherf see Tom & Enid Schantz' introduction to The Rue Morgue Press edition of *The Gun in Daniel Webster's Bust.*

The Diplomat
and the Gold Piano

ONE

The inhabitants of Manhattan are vaguely aware of that cluster of concrete and glass assailing the evening stars along the East River. The United Nations is the cause of various inconveniences, such as visits from persons like Castro and Khrushchev who tie up traffic. It also impinges on the Danish pastry industry and the clean towel services. Until this moment, however, it had had no impact on the decorators. Neither Emily nor Henry Bryce had ever visited the world assembly. They considered it, along with the Statue of Liberty, a tourist trap.

Henry and Emily were at this moment—six o'clock in the evening of December seventeenth—doing the final work on two pieces of furniture for Mrs. Camilla Lorenz. Mrs. Lorenz was one of the decorators known to the trade as the three bitches of Fifty-seventh Street. The term was a friendly tribute, an indication of rank rather than rancor. Decorating, with all its uncertainties, its exasperating female customers and its risky swift changes in vogue, engendered bad temper, and the worst tempers naturally belonged to the most successful decorators.

Henry was putting gold leaf on a spinet. It was a job he hated, and he was very good at it. The studio—the ground floor of an

13

ancient brick dwelling on Second Avenue near Fifty-fourth—
was getting cold around the edges, and he longed for a drink
and dinner.

"Let's quit," he pleaded. "What difference can it make to the
peasant who's going to play this piano whether he has it tonight
or tomorrow?"

"How do you know he's a peasant?" Emily inquired, always
able to divert a conversation from its main channel.

"Nobody with any taste would want a gold piano."

Emily rubbed her eyes, leaving a streak of blue paint. She
was touching up the beards on two ridiculous portraits the customer had ordered painted on the Florentine secretary, along
with a rose, a lawn mower, a sickle, a watermelon, and half an
egg. She looked terribly tired, and Henry felt sorry for her in
spite of himself. She was always promising things for a date
she couldn't meet.

Henry glanced down the narrow aisle between the stacks of
waiting furniture toward the front door. There he was again,
that man in the soft hat and the light topcoat. There was something about him Henry didn't like. The fellow had been there at
the door twice before in the last hour. He had made no attempt
to come in, he only looked.

"We've got to go," Henry said firmly. "There's a fellow hanging around."

"What of it?" Emily demanded. "There are always people
going by, and they see a light so they look in."

"This is the same fellow who looked in a little while ago. I
don't like it. I don't want to be held up."

"You're trying to frighten me."

"See for yourself."

Emily came over and looked down the corridor to the door.
The figure moved off.

"I don't see anybody," she said. "Please finish the gold leaf,
Henry. Rutherford will be back at six-thirty."

"Nobody believes your promises. Least of all Mrs. Lorenz.

How many times in the last ten years have you finished a piece of her work on time?"

"Henry, you cut me to the quick." She dipped a ball of steel wool into a can of brown dirt and began antiquing the lid of the desk.

"You'd kill yourself just to make that woman happy."

"I have a black mark in heaven already for helping to give Tracy a heart attack. Besides, if Mrs. Lorenz gets sick we'll have a hard time getting our money out of all this work. You know how things get tied up when people die."

"Now you have her dying. All that's the matter with her is a foul temper and a spoiled disposition brought on by a husband who pampers her and a lot of idiots in the trade who jump every time she raises an eyebrow—including you."

"That's not fair. I always maintain my dignity."

Henry gave a short tired snort, and carefully separated another sheet of the gold leaf from its protective paper, tore off a small oblong, and applied it to the molding on the piano, rubbed it flat and blew off the loose ends.

He carried on the argument without listening either to himself or Emily, a thing he had long ago learned to do, and turned to the curious question of why this particular job was so important to Mrs. Lorenz. She had been anxious and demanding many times in the past, and they either had or had not come through on the promised date. But she had never been quite so insistent on the specified time of delivery. Another curious fact occurred to him. They had never seen the customer.

"We don't even know who's going to play on this piano," he said aloud.

"We don't always see the customer."

"Usually we do. Sometime during the job. Wouldn't you think the lady would want to see what we're doing with her furniture?"

Emily thought it was somebody who knew nothing and knew she knew nothing and was willing to leave it all up to Mrs. Lorenz.

"That's not the way it works. The less they know the more they want to louse things up. 'Add a bunch of roses here, change the pink to magenta, spray it with sequins and trim it with chocolate eclairs.' "

The phone rang, and Henry took it. It was Link Simpson, an old friend and owner of the antique gun shop on Lexington at Sixty-first, around the corner from their apartment.

"I'm celebrating a terrible mistake," Link announced. "How about dinner?"

Emily agreed joyfully. "Tell him to pick us up here, in case we should be late. We don't want him sitting alone in the snow at the St. Regis."

Link didn't fall for this one. He would meet them at the St. Regis in an hour.

The phone rang again. Mrs. Lorenz wanted to know if the truckman had picked up the piano and the secretary.

"We've been waiting for Rutherford," Emily lied.

"Mrs. Bryce, I've just talked to Rutherford. He says he's been there twice and the things were not ready. I want those pieces delivered in the next half hour or I won't pay the bill."

At that moment Rutherford, the most amiable of truckmen, strolled into the studio, smiled, and sat down on a Roman bench to wait.

"He's here now," Emily told Mrs. Lorenz. "Everything will go out on time." She hung up and turned to the truckman. "How is your wife, Mr. Rutherford?"

He knew she was stalling for time to finish the waxing, and he cooperated, telling Emily about his wife's health, her interest in the church, her activities in her lodge, and her plans for Christmas dinner. His assistant, equally patient, leaned against a French armoire and studied Emily's important phone numbers scribbled on the wall.

"Who are the old gentlemen?" Rutherford asked, looking at the bearded portraits on the secretary.

"The customer's grandfathers," Emily told him.

"The Smith Brothers," Henry corrected. "They call this a fun piece, Rutherford. Do you think it's a fun piece?"

Rutherford smiled with the tolerance of twenty years of hauling decorators' creations from one spot to another in this decorators' city.

"I thought those portraits would be the end of me," Emily went on. "I can't do portraits, and I told Camilla so, but she said she had complete confidence in me. She really believes I can do anything, doesn't she, Henry?"

"We all know you're wonderful, Emily. And now for God's sake will you finish that waxing and let Mr. Rutherford get home to his supper? By the way, what's the address for this stuff?"

"I've got the address," Rutherford told him. "Right around the corner—347 East Fifty-fourth. Won't take me no time." He lifted the secretary like a box of cornflakes and eased it down the narrow corridor to the door.

Henry went into the washroom to change his clothes. He was putting in his cuff links when Emily uttered a cry of anguish.

"We forgot the hardware on the doors!"

Henry came out. "We can take it over in the morning. Get dressed."

"I wouldn't dare. If she goes over to check on the delivery tonight, she'll have an attack. I've never seen her so jumpy about a job."

"She's always jumpy. It's her nature."

Emily insisted, and Henry gave in, to save time. "Get dressed and bring a cab round and pick me up. It shouldn't take me more than fifteen minutes. Don't forget to do your fingernails. Link is easily embarrassed. I suppose the poor guy is waiting for us now."

"He's not suffering," Emily assured him. "He'll have another four martinis."

It was dinnertime and Pierre Marie Cloche, member of the Committee on Outer Space, was sick of outer space. He wanted to see his wife, eat his evening meal, and above all, cease hearing the member from Peru. He had heard that gentleman many times when they both sat on the Committee for the Definition of Aggression, a committee destined to last into eternity, eating its way through tons of paper and words, while aggression thrived undefined.

Here again they were wrestling with definition—at what point did atmosphere and space collide? The Carmen Line, Aeropause, the Gravity Theory—webs and webs of words. Of course it was all necessary, it all had to be fought out, but not, he felt, on an empty stomach.

He wanted to go home to Francine—his sweet and beautiful Francine. He worried about her, alone so much in this harsh city. As often as he could he persuaded her to come and sit through the sessions. She enjoyed entering and leaving, particularly if she had a new dress or a new hat, but the actual sitting was a terrible bore to her, and no wonder. The committee sat around the green horseshoe table like small peas in a vast pod. There were none of the diverting alarms from the gallery that they had in the General Assembly—Cubans hissing Cubans, South Africans hissing everybody. The only relief from the drone of words was an occasional secretary on tall heels stilting in and out through the panels with messages, or a mannish woman in a necktie with a briefcase coming in to sit like an archive behind her countrymen.

With a sudden frown he recalled Francine's manner at breakfast—there was a simmering excitement in her voice, in her gestures. Twice she had asked what his schedule was for the day. "You're sure you won't be home early?"

"Not a chance. The chairman wants to work straight through till seven. Perhaps later. He's a man of iron."

"He doesn't care for his wife?" Francine suggested.

She was undoubtedly right, Pierre thought, watching the chairman, whose eyes were fastened on a distant corner of the ceiling. Could Francine be planning a surprise? She loved surprises.

The last had been the complete painting and papering of the apartment while he was in Washington. He was still faintly troubled about that. Although Francine assured him it was all done at the expense of the landlord, it seemed unnatural that the owner of the building, who derived his income from rents, would go to the expense of covering their living room walls with that luxurious green silk brocade.

"Things are different in the United States," Francine had said lightly. "There is so much money. Everyone is so generous. Isn't it beautiful?"

It was beautiful, but he didn't quite like it. He hoped Francine was not planning another surprise.

He stared across the bald heads of the members to the tall windows framing the East River, the lighted oozing barges, the distant glow of Long Island City. This was the last time for many days that the member from Gaad was to feel the luxury of boredom.

TWO

Henry turned left at the corner of Fifty-fourth, passed under the awning of El Morocco, noting the spotless black and white and polished brass entrance which still came as a shock to the neighborhood, accustomed to an old brownstone in that spot.

A number of cars were parked, and others were coming in. He looked at his watch. Barely seven o'clock. Early for the night club customers. Then he saw that these people were not going into El Morocco. They were being absorbed by the apartment building he was looking for. A party, no doubt. But who goes to a party wearing a camera, a raincoat and an old felt hat?

DAILY NEWS he read on one of the cars. In his increased awareness he took in both sides of the street, and it was then that he noticed the man in the doorway directly across. Something familiar about him—the hat, a soft felt pulled down over a rather pale face, hands in the pockets of a very good topcoat, perhaps camel's hair, shoulders hunched against the damp cold, feet working a little in the snow. He had gotten wet and was uncomfortable, but didn't want to leave. He must have seen Henry looking at him, because he turned away, pulled the hat farther down, and sank into the shadow of the doorway. Not a reporter— no reporter ever shrank from the source of his bread and butter.

Henry went on into the building with two reporters and confronted a doorman whose smile was becoming slightly frozen.

"I suppose you want the Cloche apartment?" he snapped.

"Is it 4-A?" Henry asked.

"Just follow the crowd."

The elevator already contained a tall, blond carnivorous female in a green plush coat. She was urging the operator to take the car up, and he was being firm about waiting for more trade. Henry expected her to sink her teeth in the back of his neck.

"Take it easy, Felicity," one of the reporters advised. "We'll all get there in good time. What's the deal on this, anyway?"

"Why should I tell you?" she demanded.

"She doesn't know. Imagine, Callahan doesn't know!"

"Impossible." The other fellow grinned. "Callahan knows all."

Henry, enjoying these pleasantries, regretted that Emily had not come along. Felicity Callahan was part of her breakfast menu most mornings, when the two Callahans exchanged endless inanities about their private and social life, from their bowel movements to the development of the teeth, tonsils, adenoids, and psychoses of their one wizened offspring.

The apartment Henry entered, on the sharp heels of Felicity, was magnificently done. Old Camilla Lorenz had really pulled it off here. The place reeked of money, from the green silk brocade walls to the venetian glass screen. The muddy shoes of the *Mirror* photographer were almost lost in the deep carpeting. He flicked a cigar ash into a pale porcelain bowl. The cigar, Henry guessed, was to make him look older, but it gave him the look rather of a debauched baby. Everybody was here with lens or pencil in hand, except perhaps *The Times*. They might wait to see if it was something worthy or only a wild rumor.

What the wild rumor was, Henry had no idea. All he could see were milling news people and, crushed in their midst looking rather frightened, a very beautiful woman, possibly French, possibly Italian, in a very simple dress that had probably cost a couple of hundred dollars.

"Would you please stand over here in front of the desk, Mrs. Cloche?" one of the cameramen asked, almost politely.

Henry worked his way toward her, clutching the paper bag with the hardware and screwdriver. "I'm Henry Bryce from the studio," he said. "We overlooked the lock and the handle on the secretary door."

She hadn't heard a word. He disliked shouting. The simplest course seemed to be to do the job without explanation. It seemed the simplest course, but Henry had reckoned without the press. The doors of the secretary appeared to be the prime target of all the photographers. They pushed him aside to get pictures of Emily's rendering of the two grandfathers. She would be flattered. Maybe he would just say nothing and let her open the papers tomorrow to a big surprise.

Henry disliked violence and rudeness, but it appeared that violence and rudeness were called for if he were ever to get out of here. He pushed his way to the secretary, braced himself against encroaching bodies, put the lock in its groove, and fished one screw out of the bag. It would have been easier to wield the screwdriver if a heavy young man had not used Henry's back and shoulder to hoist himself to an ivory-cushioned chair in order to get a shot from above, but Henry proceeded doggedly.

"Have you caught the gold piano?" his companion said to the young man on the chair. They made their way to the spinet and were followed by half a dozen others.

The arrival of one more human being, male or female, would not have been noticed by anyone, least of all Henry, if this one had not been of a different breed. He was a tall bony man, with a homely but good face, graying hair, steady eyes behind glasses. He looked very tired, and he was carrying a briefcase. To say that he was puzzled by what he found would have been to understate things considerably. He found Mrs. Cloche among the moving litter, and went toward her. He had the look of a husband trying not to be hasty, wanting to understand, and holding in a tremendous indignation.

Mrs. Cloche met his eyes with relief and some apprehension, like a runaway child expecting chastisement but glad to be found. "I didn't think it would be like this," she admitted. "I had no idea when they said publicity—I'm awfully glad you've come, Pierre."

"Tell me, what is it? What has happened here? All these people—everything changed. Where is our furniture?"

"It's all free, Pierre," she whispered. "We don't have to pay for it. Just this little inconvenience, and then—"

"Little inconvenience!" He was still controlled, but the steam was gathering. "Who are they?"

Felicity recognized Monsieur Cloche and led the pack. They converged on the poor man, shoving him against the secretary and spraying him with questions and saliva.

"Your country is asking for a loan from the United States, is it not, Monsieur Cloche? How much of a loan? What does your government want to do with the money? What's the annual budget of Gaad? Isn't this a pretty big hunk of money to ask for, for such a small country? How much did this decorating job cost, Cloche? How do you reconcile this luxury with the claim that you're a poor country in need of help? Does your government support all its officials in such style? Or do you have a private fortune?"

The steam was ready to break through before an aggrieved voice cried, "Why isn't he black? He would show up better if he was black."

"He's half French, aren't you, Cloche?"

"Why don't we get a shot of him playing on the gold piano? That would be hot, Joe. Come on, Cloche. Just one quick one of you playing the piano."

There was a movement to gather Cloche and sweep him toward the spinet. Henry had a quick look at Mrs. Cloche's face—she seemed about to strangle—then her husband put out both arms and without a word shoved everyone within his reach toward the foyer. Something about his face seemed to paralyze their natural instincts, and they left without any real resistance. Of course some of them had been there long enough to get what they wanted.

Felicity had not been swept out, and she now advanced on Cloche with what she evidently considered irresistible charm. "Monsieur Cloche, we are all so fascinated, so absolutely intrigued with this gorgeous apartment. Could you tell us a little about your interests—what you do in your leisure time, where you were educated, how you met your wife, what you hope to accomplish in the UN—I've been looking over your marvelous library"—she waved at the wall full of books—"and I can see you're a great reader and the decorator has made books a central theme here, and it must have been your idea really—"

Cloche gradually turned on her, like a road roller ready to flatten the hot tar. "Madam, we are flattered by your kind interest. But we are very tired. My poor wife—you can see—would you mind?" He did not actually touch Felicity, but he got her to the door with a minimum of effort, and with her several men left over from the first push.

Then he saw Henry. "Sir?" he said.

"I only came to put the lock and handle on the secretary," Henry explained meekly. "We forgot, in the rush to get it delivered on time."

"On time for what?" Cloche turned to his wife.

"The surprise, dear." She was quite near to breaking down.

"I'll come back tomorrow and finish," Henry offered.

"Who are you?" Cloche asked. "Was all this your work?"

"No. We did two pieces for Mrs. Lorenz, that's all. She's the decorator."

"Perhaps you had better go—I think my wife can explain this better if we are alone. Unless you can explain for her?"

Henry said he knew nothing about the arrangements. As he let himself out, he heard Mrs. Cloche trying to placate her husband. "We'll have dinner and then I'll tell you all about it, dear. When you understand, you'll be pleased, I know you will."

He met Emily, coming to look for him, as he stepped out of the elevator.

"Where have you been?" she demanded. "I've been sitting in

that cab out in front for hours."

Emily's frontal attack generally meant she was in the wrong. "You haven't been here two minutes, have you?" he challenged.

"My nails just dried. You said I had to do something about them."

They got into the cab, and Henry noticed the man in the good topcoat and the soft hat standing across the street and looking toward the doorway of the apartment building. He must have been there all this time, watching the newsmen come and go. Who the devil was he, and what was his interest in the proceedings?

They reached the St. Regis and found Link hung loosely on a stool in the bar.

"What the hell happened?" he demanded.

"What usually happens?" Henry asked. "Emily had to do her nails."

"Henry took three hours to put a lock on a desk," she countered.

"Sit down and ease your minds, friends. Actually, I didn't mind. What will you have?"

Emily asked for her usual fruit salad *au jus*, the *jus* being vodka, and turned to Henry. "I want to know why it took you all that time to put on a little bit of hardware."

Henry described the working conditions in the Cloche apartment, and the arrival of Monsieur Cloche.

"What was it all about?" Link asked. "Didn't you find out why the papers were interested?"

"The questions were all being fired from the other side. Cloche tried to find out, but he got nowhere. The center of interest seemed to be Emily's portraits of the two grandfathers."

Emily was amazed. The work was terrible. She was no portrait artist.

"There was an attempt to get Monsieur Cloche to sit at the gold piano and have his picture taken. He was not favorably disposed. Somebody kept complaining that he wasn't black and he ought to be black, so he'd show up better in photographs."

"Where's he from?" Link wanted to know.

Henry thought some small nation in Africa. Maybe one of the new ones. "He behaved very well in the face of some very bad manners. I'd have hauled off and hit somebody. But I suppose a diplomat can't hit anybody."

"It will all be in the *News*," Emily decided. "Do you think everybody will eventually be beige?"

Link smiled. "Lucky for us it's fashionable to be pale. In terms of time in the oven, the most underdone specimen is the white man, the Arabs had maybe ten or fifteen minutes, the Malayans about thirty, the Chinese thirty-five, the Africans an hour."

This discussion reminded Henry of the man in the doorway, across from the Cloche apartment. His skin had a light creamy tone, beige really. Again he wondered about the man, but then Link said he had a problem that required the concentration of everyone present. He had become the reluctant, in fact, as-tounded, owner of thirteen Civil War cannon.

"How did this happen?" Emily inquired.

"It happened because I resisted temptation. There was a stun-ning girl at this party, an absolute Mickey Finn, and I told my-self, 'Simpson, don't tangle with her. Be sane. Be practical. She'll only give you a hangover.' So I virtuously retired to a quiet corner of the room and talked to Ferd Green, who is also in the gun business. With the aid of some insidious fluid, prob-ably nightshade, he convinced me that because Bob Abels had just bought a couple of historic Civil War cannon, I must buy thirteen non-historic Civil War cannon—from Ferd Green, of course."

Henry suggested that Mr. Green was only making polite con-versation. Where would he get thirteen cannon?

"Probably at some other party," Link muttered.

"Cheer up," Henry said. "You came home from a party with thirteen cannon. I went to a party and came home with Emily."

"You make it sound as if we weren't even married," Emily

protested. "I only asked you at that party if I could store one or two pieces of furniture in your apartment while you were in Florida."

"And when I came back, the place was so full I couldn't open the bathroom door, and the only way I could get the apartment back was to marry you."

Emily, having heard this before, did not listen. "Can't you sell these cannon to somebody, Link?"

"Sure. For Christmas. 'Get your husband this charming device for clearing the outer office.' I don't even know where I can store them."

"Look in the Yellow Pages under Cannon Storage," Emily suggested.

They were enjoying another round of drinks when Henry, gazing across the room, uttered a warning. "Here comes Camilla. Don't look up."

Link did not turn round, but Emily, amiable at any time, and after two drinks the friend of all the world, put on a benign smile and waved.

Mrs. Lorenz and her husband, Fred Wheeler, came toward them. Camilla was wearing her usual tight string of pearls to hide the wrinkles in her neck. No other manifestation of age seemed to bother her so much as the wrinkles in her neck. Her veined hands, advertising her bank balance with only one diamond, clutched the sable stole folded across her girdled stomach. Henry was sure she had been to the Cloche apartment and noted the missing hardware on the secretary. He braced himself, hoping the presence of her amiable husband would take some of the bite out of Camilla.

"I want to thank you for finishing that job," she said unexpectedly. "It was really important, I wasn't just trying to hurry you."

Henry blinked. "Were you over there?"

"No. I called Rutherford and he said he'd delivered everything he was supposed to, so that was fine."

"What was the idea of all the publicity?" Henry asked.

"What publicity?"

"When I arrived the place had wall-to-wall reporters. They seemed particularly interested in Emily's rendering of those two old men on the secretary."

"The grandfathers?" Camilla seemed puzzled.

Wheeler took her arm. "I'm famished, dear. Shall we find a table?"

She frowned. "When I'm ready, Fred … Didn't you ask Mrs. Cloche what was going on, Mr. Bryce?"

"No chance. I think you'll be hearing from her husband."

Camilla shrugged. "It's nothing to do with me."

They went on, and Emily swallowed a little more of her drink. "I don't think she's older than he is, do you?"

"Not more than twenty years," Link agreed. "Who says she's older?"

"Marie, of course," Henry told him. "Marie always thinks wives are older than husbands, if the husbands are good looking."

"Do you think he's good looking?" Emily gazed across at the couple. "He's tall but he hasn't any chin, Henry. I like that sandy type, though. His ears are too small, that means people are stingy."

"Does it?" Link felt one of his own ears. "It's amazing how I survive in this world, being so ignorant of all the important basic facts. Do you believe a lobster feels pain when it's boiled?"

"I wonder how he's managed to stay married to Camilla all these years," Emily went on. "He doesn't even show any gashes."

"What's their own apartment like?" Link wondered.

Emily said they had a big house in White Plains or Greenwich. "Marie delivered some lamps there, just so she could see it. She was disappointed."

"No gold on the toothbrushes?"

"It's sort of unbalanced—Camilla's had about twenty-five assistants and only one husband since we've known her. They all come in and tell us their troubles, and we say Quit, and they generally do."

"She's still a damned good decorator, although I can't say I admire what she did to Cloche," Henry observed. "Too lush, too insistent on display—more the Central Park West school."

"Wheeler probably doesn't listen to her," Link suggested, "that's why he can stand her. Maybe he doesn't see much of her."

"Marie says he's a very big wine importer," Emily added. "If he has his own money, and doesn't ask her for his allowance, they could get along."

They finished the evening quite late, in a small bar with music, where Emily managed to get each of them on their feet once to dance, but nothing could persuade Link or Henry to do it more than once.

They came back to their own apartment in Sixty-second Street, with the white armchairs and the cherry velvet sofa and the marble urn with rhododendron leaves.

"Henry, water the leaves," Emily commanded, as she sank into bed with her own copy of the *Daily News*.

"Water them yourself, dear." Henry began to undress. Funny that the more weary you were the harder it was to get to bed.

Suddenly Emily waved the paper at him. "Look at this!" she cried. "Henry, look!"

Henry read:

UNCLE SAM GETS TAKEN AGAIN

"Poor" African nation appeals to U.S. for loan while envoy buys gold piano, follows Marxist line.

"What do they mean, Marxist line?" Emily inquired.

There was a close-up of the secretary with Emily's two bearded gentlemen, and under it the caption: *Is Gaad pro-Commie? Marx and Engels portraits on desk of envoy.*

Henry sat down. "Marx and Engels. Emily, those were not Mrs. Cloche's grandfathers."

"Who are they? The only Marxes I know—"

"Never mind. Wait till Camilla sees the papers."

Emily didn't think Mrs. Lorenz read the *News*. She was mistaken. The phone rang, and Camilla's shrill voice conveyed the general idea that she not only read the *News* but that she had given it her close attention.

"Mr. Bryce, I want you to explain this to me, and your explanation had better be good."

Henry said he wished he could explain it, but he was completely baffled by the whole thing.

"Surely you knew that Emily was painting those Communists on that secretary?"

"Mrs. Lorenz," he said patiently, "you will remember that the sketches for those portraits came from your office. All Emily did was to copy them. If anyone is entitled to a little righteous indignation, I think it's Emily. You've put her in a rather bad light."

"And what kind of light do you think I'm in?" she cried.

He held the phone farther from his ear. "Now, look, Camilla, we'll never get to the bottom of this if you keep shouting. Who gave you those sketches?"

There was half a minute of welcome silence. "Now that you bring it up, the sketches came in the mail."

"Did Mrs. Cloche see them?"

"I don't know—perhaps not." She was becoming more reflective, and her voice fell. "There was someone else in the picture, too. I'll have to ask Julian … Oh, God, what a mess. Good night."

Henry got into bed and closed his eyes.

"Aren't you going to talk about it?" Emily demanded.

"I have a feeling we'll be talking about nothing else from now on."

The phone rang—Camilla again. Monsieur Cloche had just

nailed her to the wall. She was almost in tears, a state so unexpected in old ironsides that Henry felt some alarm.

"I think he's going to sue me, Mr. Bryce. And it isn't my fault, I don't know a thing about it, and I had no intention of doing him any harm. He says his career has been willfully ruined. By me. Oh, God."

"I can see he might feel a little embarrassment. Who do you suppose cooked this up? And why?"

Fred Wheeler came on. His reasonable tone did not conceal his deep indignation over what had been done to his wife. He repeated the question. "Are you sure you don't know where this double-cross originated?"

"I'm sure," Henry said. "It doesn't do us any good, either, you know."

"Your name is not mentioned in the *News*."

"It may be in the other papers."

"Somebody's going to be made to account for this," Wheeler said, still sizzling, and hung up.

THREE

They reached the studio at nine-thirty and Emily read off the headlines from the morning papers they had gathered on the way:

IS NEW AFRICAN NATION REALLY POOR

ARE WE SUCKERS AGAIN

PROMINENT DECORATOR DOES APARTMENT OF UN ENVOY

IS GAAD GOING COMMUNIST?

Henry meanwhile found the envelope of sketches from Lorenz. There were the two bearded "grandfathers," and the other nonsignificant items like a lawn mower, a watermelon, a fried egg, and a rose.

With the sketches was a typewritten note on ordinary white paper:

> I'd be so pleased if your artist could put a few personal silly things on the secretary. Enclosed are portraits of my two grandfathers and a list of other things that could go on it. I think the fried egg and the rose should be trompe l'oeil, on lid of desk.
>
> FRANCINE CLOCHE

"The signature on this thing is typewritten," Henry observed, frowning. "You know, Mrs. Cloche didn't impress me as a lady who would type anything, especially a signature. And would she know what *trompe l'oeil* is?"

"You said she was French. That's French."

"I know. But it's a decorator's term."

"Some female friend put her up to it. What one has, they all want. She's been around New York, Henry, if she's a UN wife."

Henry couldn't start his day until he had been to Gottlieb's Delicatessen for his coffee and Danish. Gottlieb was now conveniently established two blocks from the studio. His quarters were cramped—two tables at the back and a counter with stools at the front—but the pot roast was as tender and juicy as it had ever been.

New York was shuddering to its roots with the rattle of hydraulic drills, the Hotel Marguery had disappeared overnight, and the Ritz long ago had given place to sheets of glass, but Gottlieb's Delicatessen and Emily's studio had merely shifted from two old buildings on Lexington to two other old buildings on Second Avenue, and all was as before. The decorators and antique dealers had come over to Second like evicted cockroaches.

"We had a funny one last night, Mr. Bryce," Gottlieb remarked, wiping his hands on the great expanse of white apron over his stomach. "Some kind of a foreigner." In this country twenty years and deeply engrossed in the stock market, he considered himself a native. "Guess what he asked for?"

Henry had no idea.

"Whipped cream for his coffee! 'We got two kinds of coffee.' I told him. 'Regular and black. You want regular?' 'What's that?' he asks me. Don't know what regular coffee is. This town is full of psychos."

Henry lifted his own cup of black coffee and paused. "Did he look as if he'd been out in the cold for some time?"

"He was froze. He cooled off the whole place. Sophie complained about it, didn't you, Soph? When he came in she put on a sweater."

"His hat was wet," she agreed. "He shook snow off it, and hung it on the hook over there. His coat too. Why, Mr. Bryce? Why do you ask was he cold?"

"There was a fellow snooping around our place last night. I think the same man came back several times and looked in."

Sophie's always anxious face became deeply grooved. "You want to be careful, Mr. Bryce. You could be held up and knocked out cold and nobody would know the difference. When do you ever see a cop in this neighborhood? Just last week that poor man upstairs got a bullet in his belly because he came home too soon and surprised a thief in his own apartment. He's still in the hospital. They say his condition is satisfactory. He has a punctured kidney, a broken rib, and concussion. If that's satisfactory—"

"What did he look like—the fellow who wanted whipped cream?"

"Englishman, no question," Gottlieb stated.

Sophie's eyebrows rose. "I don't think so."

"What do you mean, you don't think so? He looked English, he talked English."

She shrugged. "I don't think so."

What she did think, if anything, Sophie did not say. This maddened Gottlieb, who launched into a recital of her bad stock market decisions.

"He always forgets to mention the Sears Roebuck and the Quaker Oats," she said, smiling calmly as she broke two eggs into a frying pan in the highly inconvenient cubicle behind the counter where she prepared the short orders. The culinary delights like pot roast and chicken fricassee were done in the kitchen a hundred steps away. There was no end to the walking Sophie did in a day.

Their broker came in, had a doughnut and coffee, and said the volume was down but prices were generally firm, and he wished he hadn't eaten the mince pie at his wife's aunt's the night before. The broker was a thin, cheerful man who wore a derby and carried an umbrella, a residue from two weeks in England the summer before last.

"And what nationality do you say he was, Friedman?" Gottlieb suddenly demanded. "He was English wasn't he?"

Friedman blinked.

"You were in here when he asked for the whipped cream for his coffee."

"Oh, that one. I'd say he was not English."

"Not? Why not?"

"I think he went to school in England. But he was a color the English don't come in. More neutral."

Henry said Mr. Friedman must have been working late to have run into the fellow.

"He was in and out from five o'clock on," Sophie informed him. "He came in maybe four times for different things. Mostly coffee."

"Do you think he was a chauffeur for somebody spending the evening at El Morocco?"

Gottlieb said he could have been, but Mr. Friedman and Sophie both thought this was out of the question. He was not somebody's servant. He was his own man.

Gottlieb snorted, irritated at having two against him. "How can you tell by looking at somebody he doesn't work for another somebody?"

They paid no attention to him and to get even he barked at a timid young woman in a raincoat who wanted the *Tribune* and had only a five-dollar bill. The papers were on a shelf outside the open shop window, and people stopping there were sharply illuminated by the five strong bulbs overhead, as they stood musing over the headlines, unaware that they were observed by the customers inside at the counter. Gottlieb served the window and the counter with deliberate economical movements, his big pink face giving gruff cheer to the scene, his large strong hands wielding a sandwich knife, seizing a blueberry muffin from the crowded little pastry cabinet, swabbing the counter with a wet rag. Henry preferred not to notice the color of the rag. The place was basically clean, but there was a marked absence of aseptic white tile. The linoleum counter was neither black nor gray, and the shelves in black were oak with the varnish worn off. It all belonged to the obsolete layer of the city, the used and worn, the still humanly small and crowded, in contrast to the vast structures that dwarfed poor, incompetent, baffled humanity. The new buildings called for a new creature, far more glorious and efficient than man.

Henry was recalled by a sudden motion from Sophie. "He's back," she said, pointing with a fork toward the window.

Henry turned. In the glare from the overhead bulbs a man outside was gathering three morning papers. There was a strong resemblance to the fellow in the camel's hair coat who had watched the Cloche apartment building last night. The soft brown felt hat was pulled down to hide a good part of his face. His smooth skin revealed no lines, but the mouth was thin and nervous, the lips moved slightly as he counted out the change. His tie, the white shirt, the jacket under the topcoat, were all expensive and carefully chosen, and the hand holding the papers was smooth, the nails manicured. A very large gold-set diamond glittered on the third finger. Henry agreed with Sophie and Friedman—the man was undoubtedly independent, probably rich—certainly no chauffeur. The clothes were too well pressed for those of an Englishman, and the diamond was not in character either. He could be European, but the clothes were American. He moved off with his papers, dropping change in his trousers' pocket.

"Is he an Englishman?" Sophie asked triumphantly.

Henry shook his head. "He must live in the neighborhood."

"If he does, he just moved here. We never saw him before, did we, Herman?"

"Who cares?" Herman grumbled.

Henry, with sudden decision, got up and followed the man. At the corner of Fifty-fifth he turned left, walking quickly, and about halfway down the block entered a doorway under a moldering marquee. A fellow like that staying in the Boulogne Hotel? The Boulogne had reached a plateau of decay, so that anything that happened to it from now on would not make a noticeable change. Henry hesitated at the door, looking into the dimly lighted closet that served as lobby. His man procured a key from the ghost at the desk, went nimbly up the narrow marble stairs. No elevator.

Feeling that he had no business to go farther, Henry nevertheless opened the door and approached the clerk. "I thought I saw an old friend come in here just now—John Burton. Was that Mr. Burton?"

The clerk shook his head, dropped his bloodshot eyes to the *Mirror*, and went on reading.

"You're sure his name isn't Burton?"

"Smith. Robert Smith."

"Sorry. Thanks." As Henry turned toward the door, he heard a smothered sneeze. It seemed to come from above, from the stairway.

When Henry returned to the studio, Claude Bernard was moving in a restless circle around Emily and her paint. They hadn't done any work for Claude for more than a year. Rumor said he was in rather deep at the bank, but he evidently hadn't curbed his extravagant taste in clothes. His topcoat, thrown over his shoulders in a manner Henry found particularly irritating, was of the most elegant soft material, and his shoes looked handmade. The tie, of course, was outrageous—a mauve silk, embroidered with a large watch, the hands outlined in gems.

"Isn't it marvelous about Camilla?" he demanded with a broad smile. "God, there's nobody I'd rather see parboiled than that witch. After what she did to me."

Henry didn't care what Camilla had done to Bernard, and he would not ask the expected question. Instead he went into the washroom to put on his levis.

"What did she do to you, Claude?" Emily asked politely.

"Didn't you hear about the Armstrong job? Where have you been? My God." Claude ran through his reserve of profanity, which served to compensate for want of masculine force.

Mrs. Lorenz had sent a Mr. Hazen Armstrong to Bernard. Armstrong wanted a complete job on his ten-room apartment. Claude was delighted. He did the thing up brown, spared no expense, the carpets alone ran to six thousand. Claude paused, waiting for his audience.

"So?" Emily asked, squinting at a white line she had just done around a panel in a credenza.

"They took me for everything I had. A forty-three thousand dollar job, and a great big chunk of it I had to put out in advance. The furniture bill from Bryant and Brock alone was twenty-two. Draperies, material, and work … Oh, God, why do I go over it? They didn't have a dime, that Armstrong outfit. They broke me flat. Ruined. Disgraced. Now I have no credit, so I can't get more work. And that, my friends, was Camilla Lorenz."

"Do you think she knew they didn't have any money?"

"Did she know! You poor innocent child. Let me instruct you in the ways of Camilla. She hated me from the day I first drew breath."

"Did she know you as a baby?"

"Don't be so literal. Tell your wife not to be so literal, Bryce," Bernard spoke to Henry as he came out in his paint-stiff work pants and an old T-shirt. "Camilla planned that intrigue as a Borgia would plan a banquet. I was the main course. Oh, God, I might as well slash my wrists."

"Claude, don't talk like that," Emily protested. "You'll think of something. You'll work your way out of it. You've been in tight places before, haven't you?"

"Not like this. Of course, if a fellow could depend on his friends at a time like this—" He paused, looking hopefully at

Emily. "If you could see your way to doing a couple of small pieces for me—"

Henry cut him off. "Why would Mrs. Lorenz want to break you?" he asked, meaning why would such a lofty figure in the trade stoop to trip such a small operator as Bernard.

"Jealousy. Pure green-eyed jealousy."

Henry restrained an impulse to snort.

"I could run a knife through her as calmly as if she were a big fat tub of lard."

"She'd be terribly hurt to hear you say that," Emily told him. "She's been dieting like mad."

A voice bellowed from the street door. "Anybody owe you any money? Don't do any work for Claude Bernard, he's flat on his back!"

August Boomer, bill collector and paternal adviser to Emily, worked his stomach and his overcoat flaps past the TV cabinet waiting to be picked up by Past and Present, and came into the light. The sound of his voice as he drew nearer was deafening. Boomer's principal collection weapon was noise—he created such an uproar on the premises of the delinquent that they would produce the money just to get rid of the embarrassing clamor. This stratagem was so effective that shouting had become a habit with Boomer and he was as loud in conversation with his friends and customers as with the deadbeats.

"Hello, Bernard," he shouted. "Didn't know you were here."

"Obviously." Claude turned his back, facing the telephone hooks and Emily's samples pinned to the calendar.

"If you'd asked me about Armstrong I'd have told you, Bernard. You decorators! Think you can do without a credit man. Do I paint furniture? Do I cut out my own appendix?"

"Easy, Boomer," Henry urged. "Claude isn't feeling very well this morning."

"He's going to slash his wrists," Emily added.

"Okay, fine, call up the Red Cross. They need blood."

"Don't be so heartless."

"A man says he's going to end it all never does anything. Me for instance, I'm different. I'm quietly eating my heart out since my wife died. You wouldn't be surprised to read in the *News* that I have blown out my brains, because I don't talk about it. I just quietly brood."

"I imagine they can hear you quietly brooding as far away as Hoboken," Claude muttered.

"What you need, Mr. Boomer, is another wife," Emily decided. "How long is it now?"

"Over a year. I tried to find another wife."

"Give me your specifications."

Boomer waved a heavy arm, causing six sheets of gold leaf to fly off the table where Henry had just laid them out. "I don't want a girl who's never been married. I'm too old to break one in. She doesn't need money—I've got enough for two."

Emily promised to take the matter under advisement, and Boomer turned to Claude with a certain sympathy. "So, Bernard, you are ruined. What are your plans?"

"I'm going to shoot Camilla."

"Good. Good. That's one way to get a roof over your head. But I hear they've taken artichokes off the menu at Sing Sing."

Claude Bernard decided his audience was not sympathetic. He left abruptly.

"So thank me," Boomer said, grinning broadly and sitting on the kitchen stool reserved for visitors.

"What started the fight between Bernard and Camilla?" Henry asked him.

"I hear a Du Pont came between them. Bernard schemed to steal a job for one of them away from Lorenz. She throws a fit. Sets out to break him. It's easy, with a dope like Bernard. If the stupid ass had just asked me about the Armstrongs, I'd have found out for him. Armstrong inherits a million more or less, but he throws it away. His wife don't believe it is gone, and she spends money like she always has. Or if she knows they are broke, she says what has this got to do with having their apartment redecorated. How much did she take Bernard for?"

"He says forty-three thousand."

Boomer clucked and shook his head. "He'll never get out of that hole. So better he slashes his wrists. Or goes through bankruptcy." He got up to go, discovered wet paint on his overcoat, and submitted patiently while Emily swabbed it with a turpentine rag. "Thank you, dear Emily," he said, and plowed his way down the aisle to the door, leaving a terra-cotta angel short a wing.

There was a lull of about three minutes, then Camilla Lorenz phoned. Her voice was strange. It had none of its usual acid, none of its imperious driving force. "Can you come over here, Mr. Bryce?" she asked, "I want to talk to you. And bring the sketches we sent Mrs. Bryce for the secretary."

Henry said he might be able to get away later in the day. He was pretty busy right now.

"You may be too late," she told him, and paused. "That man is coming to see me. I want to be ready, I must have some sort of explanation of this whole horrible thing. Although I'm not sure it will do any good," she added.

"What do you mean? What man?"

"Mr. Bryce, will you stop asking silly questions and get over here with those sketches?" That was the old Camilla.

"Well?" Emily demanded, when he hung up.

"She's scared."

"Camilla? She doesn't know what the word means."

Just after twelve Pierre Cloche came out into the winter air, pulled his coat shut, buttoned it, and turned toward Park Avenue. Manhattan smelled like the cabin of a small oil-burning tramp steamer. There was a faint odor of ocean, but it was the odor of ocean that clings to an expired fish. Francine was still crying, and still playing Debussy on the gold piano.

Francine was not very intelligent. That is, she had not the superfluous mental power that engages itself with theories and matters that are none of its business. She had enough mind to deal with the home, with his comfort and entertainment, with gracious hospitality, with all those things that embroidered and decorated life. Not enough had been said, Pierre felt, about the advantages of low but agreeable intelligence. Francine, brought up to enjoy the luxuries of a French colonial household, had she greater reflective powers, more strident intelligence, would be a serious encumbrance to him in his work. If she were capable of analyzing her own views on the dissolution of empire, the unlanding of the landed, the decline of the aristocracy of wealth, she would take a firm, stormy, and most inconvenient stand against the future. As it was, she did not see it at all clearly, or have any view of Pierre's convictions other than those of a good and loyal wife who believed it was her duty to accept her husband's position as her own.

She had cried most of the night, out of sympathy for him, while Pierre lay wide awake but still, his methodical thinking apparatus whipped about by these unforeseen and inexplicable events. He had no enemies capable of this sort of mean and small revenge—or so he believed. He had always been correct, cautious, and industrious in the interests of his government. He respected the skill and industry of the Russians, but he did not like the Russians, he did not like their philosophy. He was not the sort of person who suddenly sees Utopia anywhere, and especially not in Moscow. He believed in work, thought, the quiet, patient, continuing effort to improve man's lot. But did Washington know his soundness? He had no personal friends in this enormous, driving country. He could see himself obliterated by one flash of lightning from their irresponsible press. What was worse, his brother the prime minister could be swept out of office, and with him would go all the hard-earned reforms of his administration. The Secretariat, though sympathetic, could do nothing about the local press. Besides, they were very much tied up at the moment with another Jordan crisis.

To look back on his years of work and personal sacrifice, and feel that all of it would very likely now be wasted, made him feel cold and sad and terribly dreary.

Pierre looked at his watch as he turned south on Park Avenue. He had nearly an hour before his appointment with that woman, Mrs. Lorenz. He planned to go back and take the staff car to her establishment.

As he approached the Waldorf he saw advancing toward him a cluster of men in wind-whipped coats surrounding and running along with a short brisk figure who could be no one but Mr. Harry Truman. He had always admired Mr. Truman's forthrightness, though sometimes deploring his conclusions. He had a wild impulse to appeal to this powerful personage for help—a wave of that decisive hand, a bark from those scornful lips, could wipe out the whole ridiculous mistake and restore the ambassador from Gaad to his former secure status. "What's the matter with you boys? Can't you see this man is no Communist? Damn it, cut the horseplay and save your fire for the enemy."

He approached the oncoming cluster, he saw the fiery twinkle in the eyes behind the glasses, and for a moment he thought he actually might carry out this absurd idea, but then the reporters and the great man had passed him, and he had merely smiled. He wished he had that man's splendid political digestion, his appetite for combat.

Monsieur Cloche sighed, thinking of his shortcomings. He looked up surprised when an overdressed young man exuding a heavy odor of toilet water stopped him to ask who it was that had passed.

"Mr. Truman, I believe," Pierre answered.

"Oh." There was vast disapproval in his tone. "By the way, aren't you the ambassador from—"

"Sorry. I'm in rather a hurry." He got away, having no desire to discuss his dilemma with a stranger.

FOUR

It was almost one o'clock when Henry donned his good pants and went over to Fifty-seventh Street and the sumptuous establishment labeled *Camilla Lorenz*.

One of Emily's pieces, an Italian oval table in antique green with a marbleized top, and two matching chairs, stood near the windows. The place consisted of a ground floor for the display of some very fine old furniture, clocks, drapery materials and other ornamental stuff, and a balcony halfway back, where Camilla had her office and her center of observation.

There seemed to be no one downstairs at the moment Henry entered, so he climbed the curved stairway to the balcony. He had no preparation for what he saw—in fact, he almost stepped on her.

Camilla lay on the floor quite close to the stairway. Her eyes were half open, but the dilated pupils saw nothing. Her lips were bluish, and there was a purple line around her throat, an inch and a half or two inches wide. She was dressed in tight black silk with long sleeves, a costume appropriate to her condition. He had no doubt as to what that condition was, but he bent over her, spoke her name, felt her forehead and her wrist. Then he picked up the phone on her desk and called Louis Mancini. Louis was not only a good doctor, he was a good friend, and he could get here in a matter of minutes from his office in Sixtieth Street. While he was speaking to Louis he noted the pearls sprayed around the body on the floor. He also noted that the line on her neck was darkening.

"I don't think you can do anything," Henry warned.

"We'll see," Louis said in his gentle, firm voice.

Beside the telephone on Camilla's vast mahogany desk was a long purple scarf in heavy French silk with fringed ends.

Strange that none of Camilla's staff was here, Henry thought, and started down the stairs. At that moment a pale-eyed drone of a woman in a limp black coat came in with a paper bag from which small gusts of steam were leaking. She looked at him with some hostility. "Is there something I can do for you?"

"You're Miss Ash," he guessed at once, wondering how to put the news.

"Yes, I'm Agnes Ash."

"There's been an accident. I've called a doctor. He should be here in a few minutes."

"Who are you?" Miss Ash demanded, still hostile. "What do you want with a doctor?"

"Henry Bryce. I came over with some samples for Mrs. Lorenz."

"Oh. Yes. Mr. Bryce." Her face changed. "We've talked so many times on the phone, I feel as if I knew you."

Henry nodded. "I found her—in her office—" He glanced upward.

"You mean an accident to *her*? To Camilla?" Her pale blue eyes bulged, and she clutched the paper bag. Hot coffee began to trickle down her coat.

Henry took the bag from her and set it on a table. She saw that it was leaking, and moved it onto a copy of the *Tribune* that lay open to the story on the Cloche job.

"She's gone, I'm afraid."

"Gone? You mean *gone*?"

"Dead," Henry said finally. "I wouldn't go up just yet if I were you."

"I won't. I won't." She shrank away from the stairs. "If I had only brought my lunch. I thought about bringing a chicken sandwich—I had roast chicken on Sunday and there was enough left."

Henry wondered what this had to do with the plight of Miss Ash's employer.

"She hates to have me go out for lunch, you know. I mean she *did* hate it. She wanted someone to be here at the front during the lunch hour. Nobody else wanted to stay in, and I felt why should I always be the one? You know how the boys are— they just live for the moment they can get away." Her tone was bitter. "There was a crowd in the drugstore. I had to wait. You always have to wait. I don't know why there aren't more places to eat lunch. If I had only brought my sandwiches—" Her voice broke.

"Now, now," Henry said soothingly. "Your lunch had nothing to do with it, Miss Ash. Here comes Dr. Mancini."

Louis got out of his long green Chrysler and came briskly across the walk through the lunchtime crowd. Henry was very glad to see that quizzical face punctuated by the small, humorous mustache.

"He looks awfully small," Miss Ash complained. "Who is he?"

"I've never understood that doctors were graded by size," Henry snapped. It was true, Louis Mancini was a very small man, but that was something you forgot once you knew him. His philosophy, his intellect, and his competence gave him stature.

"Where is the lady?" Louis asked.

"On the balcony." Henry led the way, and Miss Ash trailed fearfully behind. When she saw Mrs. Lorenz she crept to the far side of the balcony, against the filing cabinets.

The doctor assured himself that Camilla was indeed dead. He seemed to take great interest in the purple mark on her neck. "Better call the police," he said, straightening up and taking off the stethoscope. "I'd say she was strangled."

"Oh, no!" Miss Ash cried.

"Oh, yes." His eye found the long silk scarf on the desk. "That could have done it."

Miss Ash began to crumple. Louis put a chair under her, drew water from the cooler and gave her a pill, while Henry phoned for the law.

In a few minutes a squad car stopped outside, and two police officers came upstairs. One took out a form and began to write. "Who is she?" he asked.

Henry told him, introduced himself and Louis and Miss Ash, and Louis gave his opinion of the cause of death. The policemen were in no hurry to convey this information to a higher echelon, but methodically completed their forms. Then one of them phoned the 17th Precinct desk, and was evidently told to keep everybody there.

Louis said he had to get back to his patients—he had office hours from one o'clock—and they let him go.

"I'll have to phone my wife," Henry said.

"Your wife?"

"My wife is also my office."

"Okay."

Emily was chewing when she picked up the phone. "What's keeping you, Henry?" she demanded. "Are you in some bar surrounded by irresistible blondes?"

"I'm surrounded by irresistible police officers—none of them blond—and the body of Camilla Lorenz."

"Say that again."

He did. "Strangled with her own scarf."

"Never mind giving out details," one of the officers ordered. "Cut it short."

"They want me to hang up. I'll be back as soon as they let me go."

"Henry!"

He had to drop the phone on her ignited curiosity.

When the precinct car arrived, Henry was pleased to see his old friend Detective Burgreen slide out of it. He was followed by his assistant, McNulty.

Burgreen spoke to the officer at the door, started toward the balcony stairs, turned suddenly on Henry. "I know you." It was an accusation.

"We've met," Henry admitted.

"Your wife is that good-looking woman with the dirty overalls and the paint in her eyelashes."

At that moment Emily, appearing from nowhere, slipped past the officer at the door, and listened to these words about herself. "I don't really think I'm good looking, Mr. Burgreen," she admitted. "Where is poor Mrs. Lorenz? Do they know yet who killed her?"

Burgreen, trying to reassimulate Emily, frowned. "How did you know she was dead?"

"Henry phoned me. We knew her so well—we've done work for Camilla for years."

"Is that so? It's nice to see you again, Mrs. Bryce, and I want to talk to you later, but just for a few minutes I wonder if you'd mind waiting outside?"

"Mr. Burgreen! It's forty below out there. And I'm not wearing woollies."

Henry took her by the arm. "Go on up to Day's and have something fattening. I'll meet you there in a few minutes."

"I'll go back to the studio," she said in a martyred voice. "After all, somebody has to keep working." With her usual luck, she caught a cab instantly and was gone.

Henry followed Burgreen up the stairs, where the detective stood for two or three minutes, studying the scene. "Anything been touched?" he asked.

"Nothing but the lady herself," Henry assured him. "Dr. Mancini had to touch her to make sure she was dead. I found her, and I didn't move anything."

Burgreen noted the scarf, the pearls, the purpling throat. "Strangling is not so common."

"It's quiet," McNulty offered. "And there's no blood. I hate blood."

Burgreen wanted to know how Henry happened to be there.

Henry explained that he had come about a job they had just finished for Mrs. Lorenz, and added, "I don't think this had anything to do with the work. At least I wouldn't like to say it had."

Burgreen squinted at him. "Anything unusual about the job? What was it?"

"If you'll glance at this morning's *Tribune*—there's a copy downstairs on the table—"

"You tell me. I have no time to sit down and peruse the paper at this point."

"The job was for the UN representative from Gaad."

"Where the hell is Gaad?"

"I'm not sure myself. It's a new one. We did a gold piano and a number of other pieces, and on one of them Emily was told to paint the portraits of two old gentlemen. Mrs. Lorenz said they were her grandfathers—"

"Whose grandfathers?"

"The wife of the Gaad man. But they turned out to be Marx and Engels."

"Kind of a smear job, eh? Might arouse a little understandable resentment in the gent from the country you mentioned."

Henry agreed. "But there were other people who didn't exactly love Mrs. Lorenz."

Burgreen shrugged. It would take time to fill in this picture. They all went downstairs and he began by having a talk with Miss Ash, who trembled and gave her answers in a whisper. Burgreen looked as if he wanted to shake her.

He got something out of her about an assistant who had been fired two months before, and who had, as far as she knew, been unable to find new employment. She also admitted that Camilla was not easy to work for and quarreled with her male employees.

"How did she get along with her husband?"

"Oh very well indeed. No trouble there."

"Same age?"

"No, I believe she was a little his senior. I know his birthday is in April and hers was in November and—"

"Never mind. What does her husband do for a living?"

"He's very successful. Imports wines and liqueurs. His name is Frederick Wheeler."

Burgreen let a little silence hang between them as he sized up Miss Ash. "Would you say Mr. Wheeler was a good-looking fellow?"

Miss Ash flushed all over. "Oh, yes. Quite."

"Attractive manners? Nice to the ladies?"

"Perfect manners. And certainly not a playboy, if that's what you mean. I never heard of his taking out any ladies but his wife."

"Thanks." Burgreen had held her up to the light and looked through her, and he turned now to a young man in tight dark trousers who had just come in. Julian Pointer was the prototype of the slender pale shadows that followed all the important decorators, each bearing his leather folder of samples and notes. A decorator who could not afford one of these young men to carry things and adjust her halo went about in humble solitude, carrying her own scraps in a copious leather bag or, in summer, a huge straw basket.

Julian looked puzzled by the assorted company he found, but not disturbed. Not until Miss Ash broke the news.

"Julian, Mrs. Lorenz has been strangled. To death," she added, not wanting to leave any doubt. "Mr. Burgreen is a policeman."

Julian turned rather green and sat down. "Where?"

"Around the neck, of course."

"No, I mean where is she now?" He looked around fearfully, as if he thought she might be lying in a corner.

"Upstairs," Burgreen snapped. "How long have you been out? What's your position here? How long have you known Mrs. Lorenz?"

Julian, confused, began to spurt facts in a high jerky voice. "I'm her assistant. I had lunch in the drugstore at Fifty-ninth and Madison, where I always have lunch. With friends," he added pointedly. "They can tell you I was there from twelve o'clock on, we had a dreadful time getting a table, the place is a shambles, I don't know why we eat there. It's the attraction of the impossible, I guess. You see so many ghastly hairdos. The coffee's terrible. I have milk."

Burgreen sighed. "I'm sure you do. Was Mrs. Lorenz alone when you left?"

"No, Ashy was with her."

"But I wasn't with her when—I left to go out and get my lunch at half-past twelve. She was alone then."

"Did you see anyone hanging around outside, or down here, during the morning?"

Neither of them had.

"She was in a lather this morning," Pointer volunteered. "Over that job they did." He waved a ringed hand at Henry. "It was all over the papers—awful mess. I can't see how they could have been so stupid about the whole thing."

"You're being a little unfair, aren't you?" Henry demanded. "We got the order from you people. Why didn't you catch the fact that those were portraits of Marx and Engels?"

"I never once laid eyes on those pictures." Julian sat down, flung one loose ankle over the other and took out his cigarettes.

"Where did the pictures come from?" Burgreen asked. "Who actually brought them to Mrs. Lorenz?"

Miss Ash said a messenger delivered the envelope with the pictures of the two men, and sketches of the other things they wanted on the secretary.

"Do you still have it?" Burgreen asked.

Henry said he had brought an envelope with the sketches, at Mrs. Lorenz's request. He'd laid down somewhere in the excitement. Miss Ash found it on a table. She was almost sure it was the original envelope—the one the sketches had come in.

"It's funny they mailed all that," Julian observed, poking his long nose over Burgreen's shoulder. "Usually Mrs. L. picked it up herself from the client, or the client brought it in."

The cancellation was Grand Central. The envelope was a standard manila one, with a clasp and glue, and bore no return address.

"Perfectly anonymous," Burgreen observed. "I think I will have a look at the *Tribune*."

Henry handed it to him, and after a moment he said the man from Gaad had some reason to be miffed. "About that scarf— was it her own?"

Miss Ash said yes, she always wore a scarf with her coat. She was wearing that one this morning.

"Too bad. I thought maybe somebody brought it along."

A taxi stopped behind Burgreen's car, and Henry recognized the tall lean man who got out of it.

Monsieur Cloche pushed open the door as if it were almost too much for him, and addressed them all. "I am here to see Mrs. Lorenz. I am Pierre Cloche."

Miss Ash started to give him the bad news, but the detective held up a hand. "You have an appointment, Mr. Cloche?"

"Certainly."

"For what time?"

"For this time."

"What did you wish to see her about?"

Cloche was annoyed, but not inflamed. "I think Madame knows quite well what I wish to discuss with her. I do not know who you are, sir, but I regard your interference as unnecessary and tiresome."

"You saw Mrs. Lorenz this morning, did you not?"

"No. I have never seen the woman. I am here for an explanation. Where is she?" His eyes rested on Henry, and he said with a frown, "Are you the man who brought the locks last night?"

Henry said he was. "I'm sorry about all this. We had no idea what was being done to you, sir. And I'm sure Mrs. Lorenz didn't know, either."

"She's in her office." Burgreen pointed toward the balcony.

Cloche bowed, strode toward the stairs. There was no sound from the ambassador when he reached the top, but he came down slowly, and he looked shaken.

"That was a dreadful thing to do to the poor man," Miss Ash protested. "Why didn't he warn him?"

McNulty looked down at the top of her head, where the part showed gray in a field of Helena Rubinstein's golden brown. "Burgreen knows what he's doing, ma'am."

A photographer and the medical examiner arrived, Burgreen took them upstairs and there was a bustle of business, during which Cloche sat down on a Hepplewhite chair and looked ill.

Burgreen returned, sat down opposite Cloche. "I'm sorry if I put you through something painful."

Cloche made a deprecating gesture. "It's a detail. One more shock, what is that, after last night and this terrible morning. Nothing but telephone, telephone, telephone, from six o'clock on. Offers to help, cries of traitor. Who is more burdensome at such a time—one's enemies or one's friends? The friends all want me to find out who did this to me. It was the Russians, they cry, it was the Belgians, it was the Chinese Reds, it was the Chinese Nationalists, it was the French Algerians, it was the oil interests of the Middle East. I don't care who it was. I'm finished. My government is put in a very bad light, perhaps will fall along with me."

"Surely it's not that serious?" Burgreen objected.

"The prime minister is my brother, you know. What I do, reflects on him."

Miss Ash made sympathetic noises, and Julian pulled a crystal decanter from a worm-eaten wall cupboard and offered the poor man a drink. Cloche accepted. McNulty watched him with keen interest, but when Julian offered him one, he refused conscientiously.

"Why were you coming to see Mrs. Lorenz?" Burgreen asked.

"What a question! Would you go to see the woman who was responsible for ending your career?"

"Miss Ash says she left here at twelve-thirty. Mrs. Lorenz was alone from that time until Bryce arrived, except for one unfriendly visitor. What time did you get here, Bryce?"

Henry guessed it was a few minutes before one. Miss Ash stated definitely that she had returned at ten after one. She had been watching the time all the while she ate her sandwich in the drugstore.

Burgreen turned to Cloche. "Can you account for yourself between twelve-thirty and one o'clock, sir?" he asked.

Cloche looked affronted. "Must I? You are including me in your tally of possible murderers of this woman even though I have never seen her?"

"Let's put it more gently," Burgreen suggested with a smile that did nothing to defrost Cloche. "I'm only trying to place everybody who had anything to do with Mrs. Lorenz this morning. Your having this appointment brings you uncomfortably close to the victim at the time of her departure, don't you see?"

"Yes, I see. The fact is, I cannot produce any witnesses to my location after twelve o'clock. I bade my wife goodbye at that time, leaving my apartment in order to rest my head from the infernal telephone. I took a walk. Quite alone. On Park Avenue. I walked a few blocks up and a few blocks down. I passed the Waldorf, but no one I know saw me. I returned to my own address where the chauffeur was waiting for me and drove here."

"Why didn't you walk here?" Burgreen asked.

"One prefers to arrive with dignity, when the occasion is grave."

Burgreen appeared puzzled, but Henry understood. It reminded him of the time Canby owed them nine hundred dollars, and drove up in a landau with a chauffeur to tell them he couldn't pay.

"You made the appointment with Mrs. Lorenz herself?" Burgreen asked.

"I did."

"That's true," Miss Ash agreed. "I heard this end of the call.

Camilla was nervous about seeing him. She wanted Julian and me to be sure to be here when you came, Mr. Cloche. I was nervous myself. I remember thinking it would be better if Mr. Wheeler were here."

"Where is he, by the way?" Burgreen asked.

"Washington."

"When did he go there?"

"This morning. Early. He ought to be told, but I really don't know how to reach him."

"His office should know," Julian told her.

Miss Ash phoned, was told that Mr. Wheeler would be back on a two o'clock plane.

A woman with a large impertinent poodle entered the shop, lifted a venetian glass bird from a shelf. "I've been looking at him for two weeks and I've decided I simply must have him," she said. "In fact I want two. One gets so lonely."

Miss Ash looked at Julian, who said, "She's all yours, Ashy."

"I'm sorry, madam, but that is the only one we have," Miss Ash told her.

"Could you order one for me?"

"I don't think so—you see—something has gone wrong—I mean, would you mind coming back tomorrow?"

"Tomorrow? I'll be in Dallas tomorrow. Surely you can take care of it now?"

Burgreen took a hand. "The shop is closed, ma'am. Now run along."

Her feathers rose. "And who are you?"

"I'm an Internal Revenue man. Boo!"

She fled and the detective turned again to Cloche. "Your wife, sir. How did she react to all this?"

"Francine has done nothing but cry."

"You think she hasn't left the apartment?"

"I'm sure she has not. She is afraid to go out. All these men with cameras. And that wicked woman with the false eyelashes and the pencil. I believe she planned the whole thing."

Burgreen looked at Henry.

"He means Felicity Callahan. She gave it a big play in her column."

"I wonder who tipped her off? You think there was a tip-off, don't you?"

Henry said it must have been arranged. The reporters were there almost as soon as the furniture was delivered from the studio. Naturally their pieces would be the last to arrive—Emily was always late. As he said this, he remembered the man in the camel's hair coat, looking through the studio door as they were trying to finish Camilla's work. Was he checking to see if the delivery would be made on time? He must tell Burgreen about that, and about following him to the Boulogne Hotel.

"If there's nothing else, I'd like to get back to the studio," Henry told Burgreen.

"I'll drop you off."

This offer surprised Henry, but he accepted gratefully. There was no faster way to get anywhere than in a squad car. Burgreen put the *Tribune* in his pocket, thanked the Gaad ambassador and took his address, told Miss Ash to let him know when Mr. Wheeler returned, and left McNulty at the scene of the crime.

FIVE

Burgreen and Henry arrived at the studio as Emily was sipping a glass of Metrecal and contemplating a chocolate eclair. She shoved the eclair under a newspaper.

"Everybody in the trade is hysterical—I can't get any work done for answering the phone. They all think she deserved it, and whoever had the nerve to kill her should be given the Congressional medal or the Betty Crocker award or something. I just called Link. He's sure it was Mr. Cloche."

Burgreen sat down carefully on a box. "Mrs. Bryce, what do you know about Moscow?"

"The climate is terrible. A mink coat is a must."

Burgreen tried another tack. "Didn't you know you were putting a portrait of Marx on that secretary?"

"Of course not. To me he could have been General Grant or Moses."

"A planned trap for the ambassador from Gaad," Burgreen observed. "A two-pronged attack—showing him as luxury loving and extravagant, with his gold piano, etcetera, and also indicating that he has ties with Moscow. The whole thing given to the press—"

"I wonder how?" Henry interrupted. "Do you think they put any of it in written handouts?"

The detective thought not. "Probably all done by 'exclusive' 'confidential' phone calls. Calculated to infuriate the ambassador to the point where he would strangle the lady decorator. Thereby completing his ruin as a diplomat."

"I don't think he obliged."

Burgreen turned a sharp eye on Henry. "Why not?"

"He seems more baffled than infuriated. He's a patient man— or at least that's my impression."

"You didn't see him this morning when he read the papers," Burgreen objected. "And after he had had his revenge, he wouldn't be in quite the same mood, would he?"

Emily agreed. "After you've tossed your cookies, you're not sick at your stomach. It's funny these people didn't come to the studio while the work was being done. Usually a decorator's client comes in to see what we're doing. Sometimes they're an awful nuisance."

"I'd like to talk to Mrs. Cloche," Burgreen said thoughtfully. "I'm not sure I have the legal right to bother her. I should get some advice on that."

"If you don't ask, you won't know. And if you don't know, you can just go ahead as if she were any poor dope on Fifty-fourth Street, can't you?" Emily suggested.

"That's the advice I was giving myself," the detective admitted, taking out a can of Galvin's Irish mixture and loading his pipe. "Have you had lunch, Bryce? I was wondering if the neighborhood offered anything besides chocolate eclairs."

"They have hot and cold heroes next door."

Burgreen shuddered. "No thanks."

Henry went to Gottlieb's and brought back pot roast sandwiches and coffee, and he was arranging these on the paint table when Claude Bernard came skipping into the studio.

"Emily, my God," Claude cried, "have you heard? She's dead. And what I said only a couple of hours ago! You knew I was spoofing, didn't you? You don't think I meant it? You won't tell the gendarmes I promised to strangle the poor dear creature? Was she strangled, by the way? I've heard seven different versions along Third Avenue. Weir says it was cyanide, Berch and Toffy say hanging, Kabe says she was shot, Orchard claims she was stabbed with an emerald-studded sword. I like the picture of her being choked best, actually. Don't you?"

Henry motioned to Burgreen to draw up his box, and gave him a Kleenex. "We don't generally give napkins, but on special days like this … Would you like to meet Claude Bernard, Burgreen? He's in the business. Knew the lady well. Hated her bitterly."

Claude looked hurt. "Who are you giving this damaging information to, Bryce? I didn't hate her any more than anybody else who knew her. What about that poor female drudge, Miss Ash? And you ought to hear her assistant talk about her—"

"Pointer?" Burgreen asked.

"You know him! Are you in the business?"

"He's in the police business," Henry said.

"Oh, my God, no! And you let me run on like a perfect fool, hanging myself with every sentence. Emily—I thought you at least had some heart—"

Burgreen bit into his sandwich. "Excellent. Glad I came. Your picture of the deceased interests me, Mr. Bernard. What made people dislike her?"

"Dislike—hell, we hated her. Didn't we, Emily?"

"I didn't."

"You're just saying that because Burgreen is a detective. You know you hated her. She was a fiend to work for, and a double fiend to do business with. She was out to break her competitors by any means she could."

Names of people who hated Camilla fell from Bernard like seeds from a maple. Everybody in the decorating business would be under a cloud, if he could manage it. A venomous man, Bernard. Whether he had the stomach for a murder Henry doubted. Still, it was an idea to keep in mind.

Emily, usually the soul of kindness, looked thoughtfully at Claude's mauve necktie with the watch embroidered on it and said if anybody had been wanting to kill Mrs. Lorenz, this was a very nice morning to do it because naturally Mr. Cloche would be suspected.

Claude drew back, clasping his chest. "And I thought you were my friend, Emily. I've always loved you. How can you say such a thing, looking right at me? And I don't even know how she was killed."

"Strangled, apparently, with her own scarf," Henry told him. "Someone who knew her well."

"Everyone who knew her at all knew she wore a scarf," Emily corrected. The phone rang and she settled into a conversation with Marie Mancini, Louis' wife. "Yes, it's true. Mr. Burgreen just came from there with Henry … You remember Mr. Burgreen—he's that cute man from the 17th Precinct. Camilla was choked. That's what we were saying, almost anybody would have liked to—but she wasn't so bad, Marie. She knew good work and she wanted things to be right, and I like to work for somebody who knows. But why did she let me paint Marx and who was that other Russian?" She looked at Burgreen who said Marx and Engels were German.

"If they were German, what's all the fuss about? … Marie, what are you wearing to the theater Friday night?"

Henry groaned. He had forgotten their date to go to a play with the Mancinis. "Better warn her that we may not be able to make it."

"What are you saying, Henry? Nine-fifty a ticket, and we may not make it? You're out of your mind." She spoke to Marie again. "I'm wearing my black coat. It's the only coat I have. I can't help it, I can't afford sable."

Claude Bernard started toward the door. "I hope you won't have any trouble collecting your bill from the departed Mrs. Lorenz," he said with perceptible relish.

"Nice fellow," Burgreen remarked, watching him go.

"He's full of little hates and little loves."

Emily thought he had more than a small hate for Camilla. She told Burgreen about the forty-three thousand Bernard had presumably lost on the job Camilla had arranged for him.

"What do you mean, 'arranged?' "

"She knew Armstrong was broke, so she said to Mrs. Armstrong, 'Claude Bernard is a wonderful decorator, why don't you go to him?' At the same time she told everybody Bernard was stealing Mrs. Armstrong from her, and he heard this, and really believed he was putting one over on Camilla. The dope."

Burgreen mulled that over. "Anyway, his performance here was excellent if he's guilty. Mrs. Bryce, how would you like to make a call on Mr. and Mrs. Cloche?"

"Just me—alone?"

"With me. I think I've found a way of treading lightly on his ambassadorial dignity. I'm investigating you."

Emily was alarmed. "I have all kinds of alibis, for any time you want to name, Mr. Burgreen."

"Of course." He smiled. "I'm only beginning with you, in order to discover who played this foul trick on a distinguished visitor to our country. There is no question of your having planned the attack on Cloche, but you were one of the instruments used."

Emily looked as if she didn't care to be called an instrument.

"We can't allow things like this to go unnoticed by the authorities. Undoubtedly bigger guns than I am will take an interest, but I'm the first on the scene, and I see no reason why I can't use this approach to find out a little more about Cloche and his wife."

"No one needs to mention the word murder," Emily added.

"That's the idea. It would be even better if Mr. Bryce could come, too. I don't imagine you could afford the time."

"Why not?" Henry asked. "We're so far behind one more day won't matter." He was curious to see how Burgreen would operate and even more curious as to how he or anyone else could possibly use Emily in a stratagem requiring the suppression of anything she knew.

Emily was closeted for five minutes in the washroom, emerged in a dress and hat and lipstick, fought her way into her black coat. "I suppose everybody will call us while we're gone. Except poor Camilla—she's off the phone forever. She'll hate that. Maybe they'll give her a phone in heaven."

There was no doubt Francine Cloche had spent most of the day crying. She opened the door, and over her shoulder they could see Monsieur Cloche in earnest conversation with two other men.

Burgreen explained that he was the detective assigned to the case of Mrs. Lorenz, and that as the furniture might be a link between her death and what had just happened to Monsieur Cloche, he was anxious to see it. Mr. and Mrs. Bryce had kindly agreed to explain the work to him.

Mrs. Cloche looked back into the living room, frowning. "My husband is engaged with these gentlemen from the consulate."

Cloche himself took notice of their arrival, came to the door, recognized Burgreen and at once asked them in. Burgreen repeated his excuse for coming, but he need not have bothered. Cloche was quite willing to see him. The two men left, and Francine showed Burgreen the controversial furniture.

Burgreen looked at the portraits on the secretary. "To my uncritical eye they look like Lydia Pinkham and Fanny Farmer with beards."

Emily was hurt. "The eyes are bad, but I did think the noses and ears were good."

"Nobody would have known these gents were supposed to be Marx and Engels, unless it was pointed out to them. So it was pointed out—the press came here knowing what to look for and photograph."

Burgreen won over Mrs. Cloche in no time, and Henry was not surprised. She was a very feminine woman, looking for something solid to cling to, and Burgreen was very solid indeed. He exuded faith in the ultimate and satisfactory solution of all terrifying situations—his slow, contained movements, his grave, kind eyes, his deference in speaking to her husband, all cultivated her confidence. She offered to make coffee, and Burgreen said that would be very nice, although he had just finished two cups at the studio. She disappeared down the inner hall.

Pierre Cloche said anxiously, "She makes very bad coffee. But she likes to play with this new electric machine." He smiled ruefully. "Sit down, won't you, please? I see you are thinking why is a man with all this on his mind concerned about the quality of the coffee his wife serves?"

Burgreen smiled back at him. "A man's habits don't vanish because he is in a crisis."

"Agreed. Worry is a universal habit, is it not? I worry, therefore I am. A certain quantity of worry, I believe, is secreted continuously and deposits itself on whatever problem is at hand, large or small—not selective, not rational, merely omnipresent. If a man were devoid of causes for anxiety, he would find causes."

Henry, studying this man, so openly suffering, wondered if he could possibly have killed Mrs. Lorenz.

"In this case," Burgreen observed sympathetically, "you certainly have genuine cause for concern, Monsieur Cloche. You have been seriously injured. Have you any idea who might feel this strongly about you or about your government?"

Cloche shook his head. "The party in power always has opposition—the party out of power—but this is a rather unusual way of showing disapproval, is it not? To endanger a loan that is vital to the whole country, not just to the party in power."

"But to make your party fail to get the loan—that would knock you out of power?"

"It may well do so." He paused, and Emily asked if she might look at the other rooms. "Certainly, certainly, Mrs. Bryce." When she had gone he continued. "Some people have been very kind and helpful. Not always those one expected to be kind, either. There is something about a suspicion of murder that tends to alienate one's friends," he added with a faint smile. "They protest their belief in one's innocence, but they wonder, while shaving, 'Did he or did he not?' "

Burgreen felt obliged here to state that no one could seriously consider Monsieur Cloche a suspect in the murder of Mrs. Lorenz. "She had a fine private supply of enemies, you know. And don't forget the possibility that her death is part of the plot to discredit you as an envoy."

"How can I forget it?" Cloche indicated the pile of newspapers on the table before him. "These gentlemen take pains to tell me everything. Even what I eat for breakfast. Mademoiselle Callahan insists it is eggs Benedict. I must tell her about my liver." He added that she seemed somewhat more vindictive than the others in her handling of his predicament.

"Felicity would be merciless to anyone she thought might lean toward Moscow, for personal reasons," Henry told Cloche. "When Khrushchev favored us with his company, she was unable to get in and out of her own house without all kinds of interrogation and interference from the police. She lives near the Russian Embassy."

Mrs. Cloche returned with a silver pot and Lowestoft cups on a tray, and Emily reappeared, her smile igniting at the sight of a large plate of fancy iced cakes. The phone rang.

Cloche got up and went to it. His answers to the inquisitor at the other end were in a low patient voice.

"Henry, why don't you get some nice cookies like this? We wouldn't have a thing but frozen broccoli if the police came to see us."

Francine laughed, and her husband, still on the phone, looked surprised and grateful. "You must come again, Mrs. Bryce."

Burgreen accepted the cup from Francine, crossed his long legs carefully, and got to the point.

"Mrs. Cloche, how did you and your husband happen to choose Mrs. Lorenz to do your apartment?" he asked.

"You are wrong," she said in her cultivated voice. "He sent her to us. To me—my husband knew nothing whatever about it until last night when the furniture was delivered."

"Is that so? And who was 'he?' "

"The president of the New York Decorators' combination—I don't recall whether he said club or association—"

"What was his name?"

Francine paused, holding the percolator above her cup. "Jones."

"First name?" Burgreen asked.

"I don't remember. I'm not sure he ever told me his first name."

"He must have had a wonderful line." Emily bit into a tea cake. "Why do people who hate coconut always get coconut? After you get Camilla's bill you won't be eating at all."

Francine blinked in a delicate frightened way. "But Mr. Jones said there would be no charge—none at all."

Cloche came back to his chair. "I told you, dear. It is a hoax. No one does work for nothing in this city."

"But Mr. Jones assured me it was for advertising, Pierre. I told you what he said. The decorators wanted to do a few apartments of UN people, for publicity. They would completely furnish and decorate our rooms, there would be photographers here to take pictures, the pictures would appear in the best papers, and that was all."

"That was all," Burgreen muttered. "Your husband was not told?"

"I wanted to surprise him." Tears hung in her eyes.

"You succeeded."

"What did he look like, the man who sold you this wonderful deal?" Henry asked. He was thinking of the gentleman in the camel's hair coat.

"I never saw him," Francine confessed. "It was by telephone."

Burgreen said that was not surprising. "Would you recognize the voice?"

She wasn't sure. She had heard it only twice.

"You did not ask Mrs. Lorenz about him?"

"No, I don't think so. He said she would come. She came, and I was so interested in what she was going to do to our apartment, that I never thought about Mr. Jones again."

Emily wanted to know why Francine had never come round to the studio, which was so close, to see what was being done to her furniture.

"Mrs. Lorenz did not tell me where the studio was. In fact, I am so completely ignorant of these things that it did not occur to me that I could go and look."

Burgreen put in a question. Was it customary for the decorator to bring his client around to the studio? Emily said it was. In fact, the client ordinarily took an active and often irritating part in the whole job. The decorator went to a great deal of trouble and expense to get samples of material, carpet, wallpaper, paint, to submit to the client. But this was different—this was a gift, so the man had said, and Mrs. Cloche did not feel she had a right to interfere.

Burgreen looked around at the freshly done walls, pale yellow paint in the dining room, a rich silk brocade in here. "How did you have the place painted without your husband noticing?"

It had been done, she said, while Pierre was in Washington last week. She had explained it as something the landlord was doing for them.

"This Washington trip—was it secret, or could you tell me its purpose?"

"My country is asking for a loan," Cloche told him. "Our embassy asked me to come down and give whatever help I could."

"Did Mrs. Lorenz know you would be away, so she could send in the painters and paperers?"

"I told her. I arranged the time," Francine explained, using a lace handkerchief on her eyes. "I have been a complete fool. I only wanted to help. I believed it would be an advantage to Pierre to have a beautiful home—a proper background. We don't have the money for that sort of thing. Gaad is terribly short of money, we must operate economically. I have no personal fortune, and Pierre gives most of his income to help maintain a hospital."

Monsieur Cloche was again taken away by the telephone, and Francine went on to tell them about Gaad, a country on the east coast of Africa so small and unimportant it seemed no one would want to harm it. Its principal products were a perfumed abundance of frangipani flowers, small brown children in magenta and yellow saris, and hundreds of monkeys that frisked madly over the roofs. Every morning at six the rain came down like stones, in a swift short shower that made everything fresh and glistening till noon. Celestia, the capital, was a favorite shopping place for tourists on lazy cruise ships, and space for shops and hotels was becoming hard to find and very expensive. The government was threatening to expropriate the outlying acreage in a perimeter some five miles deep.

Pierre, trying to listen to his wife and also to John Mullen of the Irish Free State who was on the phone, wished his wife would not talk so freely.

"Cloche, you've been the victim of a dastardly plot," Mullen said in his sad, humorous voice. "Shall I tell you where such a plot originated?"

Pierre waited, lacking the spirit for guessing games.

"You'll be surprised, I think. Not our friends in Whitehall. No sir. Something under our noses. A certain young fellow in the American group. Too dedicated. Too zealous. If there's anything in this world, Cloche, that causes trouble it's zeal for the True Cause. Any true cause."

"I'm surprised to hear you say that," Pierre could not help putting in.

"We Irish aren't zealous. We're mad. But this is a very serious young bird. Name of George Cobb. I think he is your man. He has a profound hatred for neutrals. Far greater than his feelings about Russia. Russia he can accept—after all, where's the fun if there's no enemy? Must have an enemy. But up spring these impudent fellows who say, 'The devil take both of you. Let's get on with the world's business.' "

"Like you," Pierre prompted.

"And you."

"But what have I done to this George that he should take such pains to bring me down?"

"Nothing but be neutral."

Pierre sighed. "Call me again sometime, my friend. And thank you for your kind thought." He hung up and for a moment almost smiled. "Do you know anything about the United Nations, Mr. Burgreen?"

Burgreen nodded. "During the delightful visit of Mr. Castro to our shores, I was assigned to the concourse, on special duty. I discovered they made a pretty good pot of green tea in the coffee shop, and now I make a habit of dropping in when I can. Sometimes I go up and put on the earmuffs and listen to the elocution. I like chess, and to me this is chess on a grand scale."

"Correct. That was my friend John Mullen. He sits next to me in Outer Space. When the U.K. man falls asleep with his mouth open, John takes great pleasure in it."

"And you?" Burgreen asked with a smile.

"I relish it more when France looks foolish."

"But you are French, aren't you?" Emily asked.

"Half. But I do not feel French. I was born in Gaad, I grew up there, my schooling was in England. My loyalty is to Gaad. I regard all the colonial powers with distrust, but the one I know best I regard with most distrust."

Burgreen thought that was natural. He asked if Cloche had any reason to believe this business of the furniture and the newspapers was a personal attack by a personal enemy.

"He had no personal enemies," Francine said stoutly. "He is unable to make an enemy. But the government has enemies."

Pierre gave her a look, and she was silent, flushing. He was called back to the phone. It was that tiresome Russian, the one who suffered from hay fever. "Monsieur Cloche, you have our sympathy and we want to help you. May I come to see you?"

"Thank you so much, but I prefer that you do not."

"You understand, of course, that this is a part of the United

States plot to block us in East Africa. They have been terribly clumsy and transparent—everyone knows what they're up to, and we are three moves ahead of them every time."

Pierre sighed. "I'm sure this has nothing to do with you."

The Russian was surprised and hurt. "But everything has something to do with us." He had to sneeze, and Pierre was able to end the conversation.

Emily yawned. "If there's no more blood being shed, I think I'd better get back to the studio." She gathered her bag and coat.

The phone rang again. As Pierre went wearily toward it, Francine pleaded, "Don't answer, Pierre. It only distresses you."

"It may be our own people." Pierre picked up the phone, murmured into it and listened.

While he was thus engaged, Francine said quietly to Burgreen, "He expects to be recalled at any moment. It is inevitable. And what a cruel joke. He is a good man, devoted to his country, devoted to the welfare of all men. I brought this on him. I wish I were dead."

"Now, now," Burgreen murmured. "It's not that bad. We may be able to untangle the whole thing and if he's innocent clear him in a very short time."

"He has never been a friend of Moscow. He is a genuine neutral."

"I wasn't thinking about that so much as about the death of Mrs. Lorenz," Burgreen admitted, and immediately regretted the words.

"So—" Francine confronted him with rising color. "You came here actually because you think my husband killed that woman?"

"I didn't say that."

"But it's in your mind—it's a real possibility with you!" Her eyes flashed.

Burgreen was saved by the ringing of the doorbell.

Emily, being near the door, opened it. A rather diffident young man said he would like to see Mrs. Cloche about the dishwasher, reported to be out of order.

"You have the wrong apartment," Francine said.

He looked at a pad, shook his head, and four other young men, in no way diffident, carried the first man with them into the apartment.

"Reporters," Burgreen groaned.

"Out!" Francine cried, advancing on them and waving her arms. "We have nothing to say to you. You have already ruined my husband. I should think you would be ashamed to show your ugly faces."

"Now, ma'am," the first young man pleaded, "we don't want to hurt your husband. We just thought he might have a statement to make now that Mrs. Lorenz is dead."

They converged on Pierre. Did he have any idea who might have it in for him? Did he think it was a plot by Moscow to force him into the arms of the Soviets when the U.S. rejected him? Were his friends at the UN standing by him? Did he intend to fly home to consult with his brother the prime minister? Had he been in touch with Paris on this? London?

Pierre shrank from them, but the more he retreated the more they crowded in on him.

Burgreen introduced himself, and said quietly, "Mr. Cloche is a guest of this country. He has suffered a good deal in the last twelve hours. I don't think he has anything to tell you which you don't already know. How about it, boys?"

"Oh, God, we lose more good stories by having our finer instincts appealed to. How about it, fellows, have we any finer instincts today?"

The short fat one turned to Emily. "Who are you, darling?"

"She's my assistant," Burgreen told him. "I'm leaving now and if you boys will come with me I may be able to tell you a couple of things."

They were agreeable, but before Burgreen could get them out, the buzzer sounded again, and Fred Wheeler came in.

Wheeler was surprised to find a detective and a bevy of reporters. He had come to find out more about the last job his wife had done, and to see whether Monsieur Cloche could throw any light on what had happened to her.

The chances of finding out anything with those wide-open eyes and raised pencils all around them was immediately apparent to Wheeler. He was a fresh target. "When did you get back from Washington, Mr. Wheeler? ... When did you hear about your wife's murder? ... Do you think Pierre Cloche had something to do with it? ... Then why are you here? ... Do you know Cloche personally? ... What was your business in Washington?"

Burgreen decided this was not the time to go. Emily, too, changed her mind, with new life in the party.

Henry felt sorry for Wheeler—he had the look of a man in a subway crush wondering how he is going to get out at Seventy-second Street with all that humanity between him and the doors. He accepted coffee from Francine, and dropped the spoon on the carpet. He perspired. He stammered slightly. And Burgreen never once came to his rescue, or even seemed to notice that he was suffering. He snorted angrily when someone asked if Camilla had been a member of the Communist Party—Camilla, whose life had been devoted to helping the rich enjoy their money, Camilla who owned two full-length mink coats and who had, only last week, acquired a string of real pearls.

Wheeler had an upright sort of face, Henry thought, watching him sweat. His long thin nose, his high forehead wrinkled in perplexity, his thin, strong fingers with their sandy clumps of hair, all belonged to a man who could be taking up the collection in the Presbyterian church of Morristown.

Suddenly the idea seemed to overtake the reporters that there was no more juice in the scene, and they buttoned up their coats and departed.

Wheeler drew a deep sigh and sank onto a white eiderdown couch. "Wouldn't you rather go through a riot in Celestia, Monsieur Cloche?" he asked.

Cloche, with a shade of surprise, said he would.

"Isn't he educated?" Emily stared at Wheeler. "I didn't even know about Gaad, and you know the capital."

"It's rather in the news, isn't it?"

Henry, who had grown weary of being background, asked Wheeler if he knew that Mrs. Cloche understood the decorating job was to be free.

"No, I didn't," he said with evident shock. "I'm sure Miss Ash didn't have an inkling, either. She'd have mentioned it."

"Somebody else was to pay your wife for her work," Burgreen suggested.

"I certainly hope so." Wheeler looked down at the oyster-colored silk he was resting on.

"It seems there was a mysterious third party in this arrangement," Burgreen went on, "a man calling himself Jones who told Mrs. Cloche your wife would do her apartment, and who told your wife Mrs. Cloche was a prospect for a complete decorating job."

Wheeler pursed his lips. "Camilla always checked credit ratings before she took on work."

"Who with?"

"A lot of her customers have a D and B rating. The others she found out about through the trade."

"Or through Boomer," Henry added. "Camilla didn't care much for Boomer, but she knew he knew."

Emily asked with an open smile, "Is your credit bad, Mr. Cloche?"

"It is not."

"You see—" Emily shrugged. "If Mrs. Lorenz did check the credit, the report would have been okay. So you get nowhere down that alley."

Henry was inclined to agree—the point of departure from Camilla's usually sound business procedure was the failure of each side to understand what the other expected. Unless, of course, someone else—the third party—did arrange to pay Mrs. Lorenz.

Wheeler stood up to go, said he would dig into all the available facts concerning the origin of this strange undertaking, the last his wife had ever entered upon, and the cause, perhaps, of her death.

"I'd appreciate your letting me know what you find," Burgreen told him.

"By the way, did Miss Ash tell you about the letter regarding Pointer?" Burgreen shook his head. "It seems Pointer wanted a job with Lord and Taylor, and asked my wife to write a letter for him. She did, but it wasn't quite the letter he anticipated. Miss Ash showed me the copy. Camilla was not kind, I'm afraid. Said he was a party boy, not interested in his work, showed no loyalty, had only the most ordinary ideas, but if they wanted him she would be happy to get him off her hands."

"Do you think Pointer saw this letter?"

Wheeler thought Miss Ash would have seen to that. "She and Pointer were always warring," he added. "It was a constant source of annoyance to Camilla."

SIX

Back at the studio, Emily called her mother, Mrs. Murdock, in Babylon, Long Island. "One of our best customers died this noon, Mama."

"I'm sorry to hear that, dear. Did you get the gloves for your Aunt Mamie?"

"She was murdered. Choked to death, Henry says. He was there."

"Now, Emily. Let me talk to Henry."

"It's true. You never believe me!" She handed the phone to Henry, who gave Mrs. Murdock a softened version of the recent events. Henry had a great affection for Mrs. Murdock, who was Welsh and had both feet on the ground at all times. She was tiny, alert as a bird, and had a preference for early rising, regular meals, and the Episcopal litany. Her only vice was pinochle, which she played every Saturday night with three old friends. Needless to say she had gladly turned over to Henry the hopeless task of civilizing Emily.

"Don't worry too much about this, Henry," she advised. "I'm sure it will all work out. And remind Emily about the gloves for Aunt Mamie, will you? Size seven."

Henry promised, although it was too early to expect Emily to do any Christmas shopping. She left it till the last minute, maintaining that the Christmas spirit did not overtake her until Christmas Eve.

They worked late to make up for lost time, and it was almost nine when they entered their own apartment.

Emily got into her enchanting terrycloth robe with the raveled lapels and the torn pockets, and picked up her new toy—the binoculars Link had given her after they had all been to Marie Mancini's sister's for dinner. Marie's sister lived in Yonkers on the river, and everybody that lived on the river had binoculars, but they did not use them on the river. They used them on people in the neighboring apartments. Emily longed for such a device. "After all, people live closer to us and we can see more. We'd get our money's worth in no time."

Link, sensitive to her whims, had bought her a very good set. There was no doubt she enjoyed the glasses. She could see the raisins in the rice fluffies through two sets of venetian blinds. She applied herself to her neighbors' business every night, and found it frequently more stimulating than television. Why she found it so, Henry did not know. Her reports usually came like this: "Now they're clearing the table … Now she's getting herself another piece of pie—I think it's cherry. See if you think it's cherry. She doesn't need pie, look at those hips. He agrees with me—he's telling her and she's getting awfully mad … Oh—too bad. He took the butcher knife away from her … The man that never takes his hat off is opening his mail and a can of beer. That must be an awful building—nobody uses a tablecloth in that building."

Henry went into the kitchen and shut the door. He loved to cook and he did not love conversation while he was doing it.

He poured himself a lot of bourbon with a little ice and was unwrapping the frozen spinach soufflé when Emily called him.

"Don't bother me," he muttered.

"But Henry, it's a black man in a white nightgown and a gold turban with a diamond-studded whisk broom."

"Sure."

"Come and look for yourself."

"If you don't let me alone, you won't get any dinner."

Emily was unexpectedly silent. Curiosity overcame him and he opened the kitchen door. She was at the windows, her eyes glued to her spyglass.

Henry took the glasses. "Which apartment?"

"Just above the man who never takes his hat off."

Refocusing the lenses, he swung the glass across the back-yards in the hollow of the block—a honeycomb of fences, each taxpayer jealously marking off the limits of his irritation. He took in several lighted windows across the yards in the build-ings on Sixty-first Street, saw a woman putting up her hair, and other thrilling domestic scenes, but he couldn't find the man with the hat.

"He isn't there tonight," Emily said impatiently. "You know where he lives, just look one story up from there."

Henry was forming a few sobering phrases to be delivered to Emily when he had located the proper window and found no such fantastic creature framed in it, when he saw briefly, in the flame from a cigarette lighter, a man in a white garment with a turban on his head.

"You see him now, don't you?" Emily insisted.

"It's not a whisk broom. It's an ostrich plume."

"Hair splitting. He must be from the UN."

"People at the UN don't go around in gear like that—they mostly wear Western clothes." Henry now had the curious feel-ing that the man across the block was training his glasses on their windows.

"Let me look again," Emily demanded.

"He isn't doing anything except looking at us."

"Why on earth would he be looking at us?"

"For the same reason you were looking at him, I suppose. Morbid curiosity."

Emily snatched the glasses. "I don't see how you can tell where he's looking. To me he's pointing more toward the Park Avenue side." She swung the lenses in that direction. "He's on a level with your friend Geraldine. Maybe he's in love with her, but it's hopeless, so he takes it out in watching her read *The Wall Street Journal*."

Geraldine was the name they had given the unknown female in the third-floor apartment of a building in the middle of the block on the Park Avenue side. Emily considered her rather prim, and indeed she was sternly organized. She ate her dinner on a small table near the windows, reading *The Wall Street Journal* while she ate. She always had a good-sized steak or two chops, a green vegetable, a salad and milk. When she finished, she carried the dishes to another room, presumably washed them, came back to watch television. The only flamboyant item in Geraldine's tidy little nest was her gorgeously embroidered black silk kimono. The room they could see was large and well furnished, but in no way imaginative—it could have been an office, in fact there was a filing cabinet. Once in a while Geraldine typed at a large handsome desk.

Emily thought she was national secretary to the WCTU, and very plain, but Henry suspected her curves, only suggested under the kimono, would appear to advantage in a tight black dress. If she had friends, Henry had never seen them. Now and then the bamboo blinds were dropped over the triple windows, and perhaps at those times she had visitors.

"Give me one more look at our Swami friend." Henry took the binoculars. "I think he's gone."

"What building would that be?" Emily wondered.

"It's the third one in from Lexington, that's about where Quentin Hill's bookstore is."

"You have a wonderful sense of direction, Henry. Do I smell something?"

Henry remembered the lamb chops, leaped to the kitchen. Smoke was streaming from the broiler. It wasn't often that he allowed less important matters to come between him and his dinner, and he regarded the charcoal ruins with chagrin.

"He's still there!" Emily called. "He just lighted his lighter. What on earth do you think he's got in mind?"

"I don't know what he had in mind, but what he achieved was the destruction of our dinner."

Emily sniffed. "Is something burning?"

"It has burned."

"Never mind. Charcoal is good for the soul."

Henry asked why, and Emily said what other reason would they have for hell.

"Thank God for instant mashed potatoes," she murmured. "Do you think this man is connected with Mr. Cloche and maybe he choked Camilla?"

Henry didn't answer. He was considering the effort involved in putting on his overcoat and walking down the hall to the elevator, bucking the wind in the street, trudging through slush to Lexington, down the block to Sixty-first, and then another half block to that building. He weighed his curiosity against the cutting cold of the December night, and his curiosity won. Perhaps because it was something more than curiosity—a vague apprehension, a warning that whatever was going on might be stopped, or at least anticipated if someone paid a little attention.

He didn't like the idea of this fellow looking into their apartment with those steady piercing glasses. Of course one could say it was only fair, when Emily did the same thing in the other direction, but Emily's scanning was harmless. She was not going to do anything about what she saw. But this character, scrutinizing patiently, secretly, in the dark— He rose from his chair and got his overcoat.

"Where?" Emily demanded.

"Out."

"Can I go? Not that I want to."

"No."

Henry was right about the building—Hill's bookstore was on the ground floor. He entered the narrow hallway leading to the apartments, and pushed a button at random. Someone obliged, the lock buzzer rattled and he opened the inside door. There was no elevator, and he walked up the two flights. He had no actual plan, beyond ringing the bell of the rear apartment on the third floor. Probably wouldn't get any response, unless the man in the nightshirt was expecting a friend.

He was right. There was no response. Ordinarily it would not have occurred to Henry to try the door—all doors were snap-locked. But he did try this door, and he was not altogether pleased to find it opening under his hand. This is a trap, he thought, but he moved cautiously in, his hand still on the doorknob. Nothing happened. He paused, listening. No tiny sound conveyed the presence of a second person. The place was cold, with the damp chill of empty rooms. In the light from the hall he could see bare floor, bare wall. Beside him, near the door frame, was the light button. He was reaching for it when suddenly strong fingers snapped around his ankles, jerked him off balance. He fell to the floor and lay there expecting a blow. Instead, a pair of trousered legs stepped over him, the door closed, and leather soles tapped quickly down the public corridor to the stairs.

Henry got up, feeling foolish. No use trying to run after him and see who it was. He wasn't that athletic. He turned on the light, a glaring bulb in the ceiling, and looked around him. It was a room-and-a-half arrangement, all the windows overlooking the inside of the block, with an archway between the larger room and the kitchen-dining alcove. There was not a stick of furniture anywhere, not so much as a box of pepper in the cupboards over the gas stove. No one lived here. The catch was left on the lock so that someone could get in and out, without the formality of owning a key. Someone merely wanted to use the apartment as an observatory.

Henry opened a door, discovered the bathroom. The basin was still wet and had a rim of greasy black. This same greasy black decorated a cake of green soap.

Thinking this over, Henry looked into the only closet. On the floor was a crumpled sheet. He lifted this, and found three safety pins, the gold turban, and the jeweled ostrich plume.

He had no desire to linger on the scene. As he snapped off the light, he noticed a smudge of greasy black on the white wall.

When he got back, he found Emily washing the dishes, an

absolutely unknown phenomenon. "Get out of my kitchen," Henry ordered.

"I didn't think you'd be back," she explained, drying her hands on a dish towel. "I wanted the place to look neat for the undertakers."

"I found out something. Our friend is not black. He paints himself black after he gets there, and washes it off when he leaves. Also, he doesn't wear his nightgown out on Lexington Avenue. And there was a gold turban with gems."

"Real?"

"Fake."

He told her about the attack on his ankles.

"Henry," she cried, "you probably just saw the murderer!"

"What makes you think so?"

"You said he had very strong hands. And Camilla was strangled." Emily looked at him closely. "Didn't you think of it before? You're shivering. I'll make you a drink, Henry."

"All right," he said. "Remember to put liquor in it."

Emily called Link and reported this development. "What do you think?" she demanded.

"I think the binoculars were a good investment."

Emily gave him a summary of their visit to Pierre Cloche, and then Henry took the phone and injected some order into the script of that event.

"Do you think Cloche strangled Camilla?" Link asked.

"I don't know. But the publicity about his apartment was carefully planned. Somebody told his wife she could have her quarters decorated free if she were selected by this phony nonexistent decorator's organization."

"That old photographer's gag? 'You are one of six people chosen to receive a free portrait of your little boy, in our publicity campaign in your city. Just return the enclosed postcard and receive absolutely free—' God, she must be gullible," Link concluded.

"I think she is," Henry agreed. "And charming. I feel terribly sorry for both of them. He seems like a high type."

"Does Burgreen share this view?"

"I don't know. He's not interested in who threw the mud at Cloche—he only wants to find out who killed Mrs. Lorenz."

"Suppose it's the same person?"

Henry paused. "Why?"

"As a clincher. In case the strange portraits on his furniture weren't enough to discredit him, make him appear guilty of murder. He'd have to be recalled then. His government would have no choice."

Henry thought it was going pretty far, just to accomplish a change of ambassadors to the UN.

"We don't know what the reason is—what the stakes are."

Emily borrowed the phone. "Link, can't you have dinner with us and Marie and Louis on Friday? Maybe we could get you a ticket for the show, too—a cancellation might come in."

Link's refusal was explosive, and Emily looked hurt. Marie Mancini was her best friend. She turned to Henry. "Link wants to know what the play is."

"I don't know. I thought you knew."

"Marie picked it out and got the tickets. She said the Baroness Arlotto raved about it."

Henry had a feeling it would be a bad evening.

About ten o'clock on Thursday morning Henry announced that he was going over to the Lorenz establishment to find out how the outstanding bills were to be handled, and whether he had to submit extra copies for the executor.

"Camilla isn't cold yet, Henry. I think it's very bad taste to go over there and talk money at a time like this."

"She can't hear me. And I don't imagine Wheeler will be there. If he is, I won't talk money, I'll just express sympathy and leave."

"You just want to snoop."

Henry did not attempt to refute so crass an accusation. When he reached the shop, he found Julian Pointer and Miss Ash in a heated argument. There was a natural antipathy between them—Miss Ash had a strict belief in duty, probity, punctuality, and the life eternal; Pointer regarded these items as useless baggage brought along in the bottom of the ancestral trunk. Also, he felt contempt for a woman who had not succeeded in marrying, and she disapproved of a man who did not want to marry.

"You got back before I did," Pointer was saying in a loud voice. "You had plenty of time to pick up a pocketful of the pearls."

"I did not go up to the balcony until they asked me to—there was a policeman with me when I did go."

"If you ask me, I think you came back early and found her first—if you didn't—"

It was here they became aware of Henry, who pretended to have heard nothing, and said he wanted to know where to send the studio bill for the Cloche work.

"Miss Sackcloth can tell you that, Bryce," Pointer said shortly, and moved off.

Henry and Miss Ash discussed the account, and then he said, "They weren't real pearls Mrs. Lorenz was wearing at the time of—at the time?"

"Yes, they were."

"And didn't you find them all?"

"That policeman says there is a pearl missing. I'm sure I don't see how that could be. If the person who killed Mrs. Lorenz wanted pearls, he would take all of them, wouldn't he?"

Henry agreed. "How did Burgreen come to the conclusion that one pearl was gone?"

"He had me string all that we found on the original cord. Then he checked with Tiffany. The pearls were new, you know. Mr. Wheeler gave them to her for their anniversary on the eighth. He always bought her lovely presents. Poor Mr. Wheeler."

"Poor Mr. Wheeler," Pointer mocked, taking his overcoat from a hanger at the back. "Lucky dog, I'd say." He left the shop.

Miss Ash was glad to see him go. "When you think about a murderer," she reflected, "you say he would do so and so, because you in the full possession of your faculties would do so and so. But a murderer is not necessarily in his right mind, is he?"

Henry smiled. "All the same, I can't see him taking one pearl after he did the job. What did Burgreen make of it?"

"He did not communicate what if anything he made of it. At least not to me."

Henry studied her for a moment, decided to ask a direct question. "Do you think Pointer killed her?"

She was alarmed. What Miss Ash wanted was the luxury of suspicion and innuendo, without the responsibility of accusation. "I haven't said anything like that, Mr. Bryce. But Mr. Pointer was not at all loyal to Camilla. He said dreadful things about her to other decorators and to wholesalers and shopkeepers—people have told me."

"These young assistants always talk that way, don't they? They accuse their employers of stealing their ideas, working them to death, and paying them less than Fagin's juvenile pickpockets."

Miss Ash looked at him. She had a disconcerting habit of turning on a stare and forgetting to turn it off while she did further thinking. He noticed that she had a faint odor of sweat, and her skin was quite oily. She wore brown and gray, and had the general appearance of a horehound. He wondered how Camilla had put up with her. Probably having Miss Ash around made Camilla feel young and dazzling. And then Miss Ash was a demon for work, and very loyal.

"Do you know who arranged for the Cloche job?" he asked.

"As I told Mr. Burgreen, the whole thing was arranged by telephone. A man called, saying he was Monsieur Cloche's personal secretary, and that they wanted Mrs. Lorenz to do the apartment. Full instructions would be sent over by messenger, which they were, with a substantial sum in cash, as an advance. This isn't usual, you know, but the man said Monsieur Cloche didn't want to write checks in case there might be an investigation by his countrymen into the cost of the decorating."

"That eliminated the danger of having Mrs. Lorenz investigate Cloche's credit, which might have tipped him off to what was happening," Henry concluded.

Miss Ash had that stare again. She whispered, "Did you know about the letter?"

"What letter?"

"The letter Mrs. Lorenz wrote to Lord and Taylor about Julian. He wanted to find another job, you know. Desperately. He thought she'd recommend him, but she told the truth. He was raving—simply raving. I'm sure he wanted to kill her, Mr. Bryce."

"How did he find out about the letter?"

She flushed. Evidently Wheeler was right, and she had made sure Pointer saw the letter. Not a very sweet character, Miss Agnes Ash.

Henry told Burgreen about this conversation when he called the studio later in the afternoon. "I wouldn't want her boiling my oatmeal," Burgreen agreed. "She's a sly one."

"What does Homicide think about Camilla's death?" Henry wanted to know.

"They see it as Cloche, no question, and they don't like the sticky international complications. They think if we give his government a few days, he'll be recalled, and that will end everybody's embarrassment."

"And suppose it isn't Cloche?" Henry suggested. "Why are they so sure?"

"Maybe because I told them it was."

"Are you really that convinced?"

"Let's say I'd like to be that convinced."

Henry objected. "You saw the kind of man he is, Burgreen. He's no murderer."

"He's a patriot. Who knows what a patriot will do for the good of mankind? Kill Lincoln, blow up a kindergarten—"

SEVEN

"Why did she have to get herself killed just before Christmas?" Emily complained on Friday morning. "All this work ahead of us, and no time to enjoy the excitement. I've got to get a dress for tonight, and have my hair done."

The front door slammed and Henry looked up to see Claude Bernard springing down the aisle on his toes like the Deerslayer.

"Mr. Bernard," Emily greeted the new arrival with cool surprise. "How interesting that you should be calling on us every day now. What's the attraction?"

"I've always been terribly fond of you, Emily darling. Any more on Camilla?" He seemed, Henry thought, frothing with some inner excitement.

"Nothing new, except the man spying on us in a sheet and a gold turban."

"You're kidding."

"I'm not. His observatory is across the block in the building where Quentin Hill has the bookstore."

"Are you sure he's looking at you?" Bernard inquired. "Maybe he has a girlfriend in another building."

Emily began to assemble her lunch—a bowl of raisin bran, a container of coleslaw, and a dill pickle. "Will you boys join me?"

"I'd rather have gin and cold gravy," Henry said. "Claude,

did you ever see anyone take whipped cream in coffee?"

"Yes, in Brussels. I was there last summer looking for old junk and I never saw so much whipped cream in my life. They rub it in their hair."

"Maybe my beige man in the camel's hair coat is a Belgian."

"You and that beige man!" Emily complained. "It's a fixation."

"I wonder if he's somebody from the UN who has it in for Cloche?"

"I don't want you going over there to look for him," Emily warned. "The place is wired for murder."

They looked at her.

"Those headsets," she explained, as if anybody ought to know. "A Russian just crosses the wires, and phizz! you're electrocuted."

Claude looked at his watch. "How is Gottlieb's pot roast these days?"

Henry said it was still excellent, and Bernard went off.

Emily said, "I think he's hatching something, Henry."

"What could he hatch? He's as menacing as a mashed potato sandwich."

But Emily was right. Claude Bernard had a plan. He was thinking about it as he walked toward Gottlieb's. It was a plan that made him shiver when he thought of the next step in its execution, but he was determined to take that step. First he must make the phone call.

He entered Gottlieb's delicatessen and found comfort in the tranquil customers munching at the counter. He wriggled onto a stool between a cab driver and a messenger with an envelope.

All morning Bernard had had the feeling that he was on top of things at last, that this was his hour and he had only to exercise caution and judgment to get what he wanted. As he ate the substantial pot roast sandwich and drank the hot black liquid, his courage increased. Halfway through his coffee he got up with sudden resolve. "Don't take it away. I'll be back," he said to Sophie.

He made the call. Between the dropping of the dime and the sound of the responding voice, perspiration ran down him, but he conveyed his message. There was unexpected compliance at the other end. He returned to the counter with a feeling of exhilaration. The messenger on the stool at his right was giving Gottlieb a bad time about the coffee. If Claude had been less engrossed in his own undertaking he would have noticed that Gottlieb was handling the fellow gently.

Irritated, Claude said, "Shut up and stop being an ass."

The young man turned on him. "Who asked for your opinion, you pansy in the purple necktie?"

Claude froze.

"Come outside and I'll knock your damned head off!"

"Now Melvyn," Gottlieb pleaded, "be nice. Don't annoy the gentleman." The words glanced off. Sophie, coming in from the kitchen, added hers, to no avail.

Melvyn's fuse had been ignited. Suddenly he picked up the heavy glass sugar container and leaned toward Bernard. Claude shrank, feeling sick. He was not possessed of much physical strength, and to take on this maniac was unthinkable.

Sophie looked at Gottlieb, and Gottlieb came slowly out from behind the counter. "You'll have to go now, Melvyn. That's enough. You'll have to go." No one at the counter offered to help Gottlieb. There was a long moment of silence. Then Melvyn slid from the stool and moved toward the door, shouting threats.

When he had finally taken himself away, Gottlieb turned to Bernard. "We wouldn't have let him touch you. I had my hand on the butcher knife."

"Thanks," Claude whispered, and he picked up his cup with a shaking hand. Sophie urged him to have a bowl of soup, but he refused. He left the place, started up Second Avenue on foot.

He was fearful now that he would not be able to carry it off. In a thing like this, everything depended on nerve, and his nerve was suddenly gone. If it was a big, well-planned operation—

and he felt that it was—he would be sucked under the wheels like a barking dog.

He saw vividly and sadly how everything depends on chance, a mere nothing deflected you—a glass of cold milk at lunch, lying leaden in your stomach, canceled action at the second when action was essential.

Feeling the slap of cold sleet on his cheek, Claude shivered and wished he had not made the phone call. That was the hinge on which the thing turned now. He must go on, because they knew who he was. He tried to digest the unsettling incident by viewing it impersonally. New York was a sort of Coney Island, in which the steam could suddenly roar up from the floor, and the floor itself drop out from under you, while the wavy mirrors of the gossip columnists showed all the inhabitants to be grossly deformed. He thought about Felicity Callahan, who had helped in her small way to bring about the present advantageous circumstances—advantageous to Claude Bernard. It was a beautiful moment for him, and he must not be shaken by a mere accident. At stake were all the things he loved—ease, color, gaiety, good times and bright talk. He must not let them go out of fear.

Nevertheless, as he stopped a cab and fell into it, he was perspiring and very cold.

At three Emily was trying on a black creation in Bloomingdale's.

"It seems a little tight," she said as the clerk pulled and hauled in the region of her hips.

"Madame, if you wouldn't mind a suggestion?"

"I'm already taking Metrecal, if that's what you mean. It doesn't seem to do a thing."

"I was really thinking of a better foundation garment—something that would do more for your figure. We get in the habit of wearing a certain type garment, and you know how it is—"

Emily looked at herself. "If you think so," she conceded.

There was more pulling and hauling, mixed with perspiration on both sides, and after an hour of supreme sacrifice there was a transfer of assets from Emily Bryce to Bloomingdale's. Emily emerged with a box under her arm, caught a taxi to Yolande's.

"Your friend Mrs. Mancini was here," Yolande told her. "I did a beautiful job on her. She said you were all going to the theater this evening—big night. Nine-fifty for tickets."

"And dinner at Leo's," Emily added. "Who owns the building on Sixty-first where the bookstore is?"

"Quentin Hill's bookstore? He does. I can't stand him. Snoopy. Always knows who's sleeping with who."

Emily had the pleasure of telling Yolande about the man in the sheet.

"My God, Mrs. Bryce! Isn't it awful the way New York is changing? You never would of had a thing like that in the old days. All these foreigners, eating artichokes and stabbing people in the subways. Why do you think this fellow was watching your apartment?"

"He thinks we have the papers," Emily told her.

"The papers?"

"Did Marie tell you what the play is?"

"No, she didn't, Mrs. Bryce. At nine-fifty a ticket, don't you know what you're going to see?"

Emily smiled, and settled under the dryer.

An hour and a half later she picked up Henry and they went home.

"Do you think he's watching us now?" Emily asked, as Henry unlocked their door.

"I'll see. You get dressed."

"You have all the fun," she grumbled, going into the bedroom with her new girdle and dress. Henry turned the binoculars on the windows of the third-floor apartment in Mr. Hill's building. The window was dark, and seemed to be empty. He waited for the flare of a cigarette lighter.

"Is he there?" Emily called.

"No. Not a sign of life."

"That's funny. Do you think he found out whatever he wanted to know last night?"

"What could he learn from our activities last night? We didn't do anything. Nobody came to see us."

"You'd better get the liquor and glasses out, Henry. They'll be here any minute."

"All right." He continued to watch the dark window, but no lighter flamed.

"Henry, I'm stuck!" Emily called.

Henry had just zipped her into her new black dress when the Mancinis arrived.

Marie made her entrance without words, allowing her diamonds and her full-length mink to speak for themselves. Emily gave out appropriate sounds, but Henry found it impossible to be enthusiastic when enthusiasm was so obviously expected. He took Louis to the kitchen while he made the drinks.

"They mean well, women," Louis muttered. "Just don't pay too much attention to them."

Henry supplied Marie and Emily with old-fashioneds, although they were under full steam without fuel.

"I told Louis to get my diamonds from the bank yesterday but he always puts it off," Marie complained. "He's afraid we'll be robbed in the night, and this afternoon he had a patient at the last minute—some old man with a hernia—wouldn't you think they could have their hernias in the middle of the week? No. Always on Friday. Never Monday or Tuesday for a hernia or a heart attack. So guess what Louis said? He said can't you go to the theater without the diamonds this time? Imagine!"

"I only thought there might be ladies who don't always wear their diamonds," Louis explained mildly.

Marie gave him a look of pity. "Who has diamonds, wears them." She turned to Emily. "What are you wearing tonight?"

"What I have on." Emily looked down modestly at her new black dress.

"Oh. Well, you can't always be buying something every time

you go out. Where did you see the man with the spyglass looking at you?" Marie went to the window and pulled back the
curtains. "Maybe he's there again."

"He's not there tonight," Henry told her. "I looked."

"Do you want to see Henry's girl friend?" Emily asked, taking the binoculars and scanning the Park Avenue side of the
block. "She's there."

Marie accepted the glasses and was guided to the bay window on the third floor. "That one? Plain. Very plain. I'm surprised at you, Henry."

"It's her money I like," Henry explained.

Marie became more interested. "There's a man—she's talking to a man!"

Emily wanted the glasses. "We've never seen a man in her
apartment. Henry, do you approve?"

Henry didn't give a damn.

Emily made a strangling sound. "Henry! The man is Claude
Bernard!"

"Really?" Henry was not terribly interested in a view of
Claude Bernard, through binoculars or any other way, but he
got up and looked. He saw Claude. Then he saw the other man,
a medium sized man, with his back to the windows. He was
wearing a camel's hair coat.

Henry wished the fellow would turn around, but he kept his
back to the windows, perhaps by design. Then abruptly the girl
let down the bamboo blind and the scene was finished.

"Too bad," Emily said. "Do you think it's romance or business?"

"It's the other man I'm curious about," Henry remarked.

"What other man?" Marie demanded. "I didn't see any other
man, did you, Emily?"

Emily had not. They accused Henry of loading his own drinks.

"I had one average bourbon. That was the man I saw hanging
around the studio while we were finishing those pieces for the
Cloche apartment. When I went over to the apartment with the

hardware, there he was, lurking across the street watching the reporters swarm. The morning after the Cloche affair, he came by and picked up all the morning papers at Gottlieb's, and I followed him to the Boulogne Hotel—"

"The Boulogne!" Marie was scornful. "He can't be important if he stays at the Boulogne."

"How do you know it's the same man?" Emily demanded.

"He was wearing a camel's hair coat."

"Did it occur to you that there might be two camel's hair coats in New York?" Marie asked.

"Naturally. But I'm almost sure it's the same man. His appearance, manner, stature—everything. If he'd turned around so I could see his face, I'd be absolutely sure. He has a beige complexion."

"Beige?" Louis was amused.

"Yes, beige. Very smooth skin, without wrinkles."

"It was inevitable. Everything man wears, sits on, or looks at is beige. He was bound to take on protective coloration sooner or later. Do you think this fellow is the first of the race to show the change?"

The blood rose in Henry's neck. "All right, all you smart people, I'll prove it. I'm going over there and wait in a taxi till he comes out of that building."

"Henry," Emily cried. "We're going to dinner at Leo's."

"That man might be in her apartment all night," Marie added.

"People take off their coats for romance," Henry told her. "He'll be coming out soon. Suppose I meet you all at Leo's."

Louis vetoed that. Henry might be gone some time on this mission. They'd better all meet at the theater.

"I'm going with Henry." Emily picked up her mink stole and her bag.

"Who's going to take care of the guests?"

"They know us well enough to cancel Emily Post during an emergency. Anyway, we'll be at Leo's before they are."

Emily was wrong. They waited in a taxi outside Geraldine's

building. In a few minutes the beige man emerged with a heavy cowhide bag, got into a cab.

Henry spoke to his driver, and they pulled into traffic.

"Are you going to follow him? What about dinner?" Emily asked, but her eager eyes were fastened on the car ahead.

They turned right into Sixty-second, and Emily said maybe Henry's beige man was going to Claude's apartment, which was in the building across from their own.

"He wouldn't take a cab for a little ride like that. And he'd bring Bernard with him, I should think."

"What's in that heavy bag?" Emily wondered. "Maybe he took Geraldine's silver."

"Not very likely. Claude was there all the time."

"A lot of protection Claude would be."

The traffic was not at its evening peak, and their driver was able to keep the beige man in sight. They crossed town to Second Avenue, turned right again and entered the easy fast flow of vehicles downtown. Everybody reined in for the lights at Fifty-third, and there the man in the camel's hair coat looked back. He and his driver had a hasty consultation, and when the lights turned, they shot ahead recklessly.

"Damn," Henry muttered. "He knows we're following."

"He'll try to shake us now," the driver agreed. "Hold your hats."

The first maneuver was west on Forty-ninth. That didn't shake the pursuers, so there was a double back on Fifty-second, and then it became clear they were making for the Queensboro Bridge through one of the devious narrow channels approaching it from the Manhattan side.

"Want me to follow across the bridge?" the driver asked, though how he could do anything else now was not clear.

Henry urged him on.

"Why is he coming over here?" Emily demanded. "I think he's leading us into a trap."

"No, he's just trying to dodge us," the driver explained. "Do you know if he carries a gun? I don't want to get shot before I get my Christmas club money out of the bank."

Henry didn't believe he would do any shooting. During the next half hour they took a screeching tour of some of the most uninteresting streets in the world, and then headed back toward the bridge. But they did not reach the bridge. Somehow, and Henry never knew just where, they got onto a road that led to one of the islands in the middle of the East River. The island seemed to be more or less deserted, although it had a number of concrete buildings and a maze of narrow snowy roads.

"I don't like this," Emily confessed, getting closer to Henry and looking out at the unfamiliar dark shapes. "My feet are freezing, and I'm hungry, and maybe it isn't the same man at all."

"If it isn't the same man, he's going to an awful lot of trouble to keep us from our dinner. He has something on his mind he doesn't want to share with us."

"It's not on his mind, it's in that cowhide bag."

The driver, too, was becoming uneasy. He asked again about the possibility of gunplay. "Nice spot for an ambush," he pointed out as they skidded around a low wall.

Henry said nothing, but he had a distinctly cold feeling down his spine, and his hand was on the door handle. They couldn't see the other car now, and their driver slowed, got caught in a slippery drift, and the wheels spun.

Henry could see panic in his hunched shoulders and gripping fingers. "Let me try," he offered. "I come from upstate where we get a lot of this."

The driver was skeptical, but he slid over and let Henry get behind the wheel and rock the car. Emily gave advice.

"Keep quiet and get out and push," Henry ordered.

"In my velvet pumps?" she wailed, but she got out, just as Henry succeeded in working free of the rut.

"Get in, hurry up, we'll lose them," he shouted.

In a moment they were off the island and back on the bridge, with Henry still at the wheel.

"If we get picked up, I'll lose my license," the driver warned.

"Just let me have it till we catch him at a light."

Emily looked down the river from the bridge to the UN building, glittering in many of its corners with late lights. "Maybe poor Mr. Cloche is sitting in one of those pigeonholes biting his nails," she said.

They caught the other car at a light shortly after they crossed the bridge, and Henry and the driver changed places. Perhaps the two men instead of one in the front seat had confused the man in the camel's hair coat. At any rate, there seemed now to be no attempt to lose them—just a fast trip downtown on Second to Thirty-eighth. Here the other cab turned left and proceeded more slowly.

"Take it easy," Henry said. "I think they're going to stop."

They followed at a distance, saw the man get out with his heavy bag and dismiss the cab. He crossed the walk and disappeared inside an ancient red brick dwelling.

"Stop a minute," Henry said. "I want to get a good look at the place."

The ground floor of the building was given over to a hairdressing establishment, May's Beauty Salon. A dim light came on inside and they could see that the curtains were yellow and red flowered cotton. Display cards in the door glass proclaimed the wonders of various tints and sprays. There was a drift of dirty papers in the doorway.

"I don't think May is in business any more," Emily observed.

Henry opened the cab door.

"Where are you going?"

"I want to see what he's doing in there."

"Are you tired of living, Henry?"

"Wives," he muttered, but he allowed her to pull him back. The street was deserted and the building had an unwholesome aspect—perhaps it would be wiser to investigate in daylight.

They entered the Music Box Theatre with a bag of hamburgers and settled damply into seats beside Louis and Marie. Emily removed her soggy pumps and Henry opened the program. The play was *Down the Drain* by Graham Graham.

"What did we miss?" Emily whispered to Louis.

"Egbert was trying to hang himself in the coal shed."

"Was it love?"

"They didn't say. He was seven."

"Maybe it will pick up in the second act." Emily opened the crackling paper bag and took out a hamburger.

"You can't eat that here," Marie hissed. "Didn't you have dinner?"

Emily shook her head. "Have a pickle?"

The curtain rose on a cellar.

"Where are we?" Emily whispered.

The man in front turned to glare, and Louis said quietly this was Egbert's home in Sussex. Egbert, now a grown man, appeared to be working on a clogged drain with a toothbrush.

"Why doesn't he use a long wire?" Emily demanded.

The man in front turned. "Why don't you go back to kindergarten?"

The hero's mother descended the cellar steps, carrying a bowl of lentil soup, and Egbert pretended to be grateful but as soon as she disappeared upstairs he put the lentils down the drain, thereby compounding his plumbing difficulty. A girl came to the head of the stairs, stopped.

"Come on down," Egbert said.

"No."

"Oh, come on."

"No. I'm afraid."

"Of me?"

"Of toothbrushes."

"Eleanor! I always supposed you felt nothing. Now I know. You share the Human Condition. Eleanor, I love you."

"I love you, too, Egbert. But I cannot bear the sight of you."

Emily leaned toward Marie. "Are you sure this is a comedy?"

Marie didn't like the play, but as she had chosen it on the advice of the Baroness Arlotto, whose husband was descended from the great Italian poet, not to like it was a reflection on Italian taste and culture. "Try to understand it," she ordered.

"I'm trying," Emily said meekly.

The next scene got the hero out of the cellar and into the living room, where he finally brought himself to tell his mother that he did not care for lentils, and had never cared for them, whereupon they had boiled mutton for dinner.

"Why are they eating dinner in the living room?" Emily demanded.

"His uncle sleeps in the dining room."

"Why?"

"Because he's afraid of birds and there is a robin that looks in his bedroom window every morning."

In the third act Egbert went to the attic, and made a speech, declaring that the Almighty presented us all at birth with a lovely plaything—Life—in the form of an open safety pin, which we promptly swallowed, thereby insuring lasting enteric difficulties, or the Human Condition.

Henry began to think about Geraldine. She apparently knew the man in the camel's hair coat. He was tied up with the Cloche affair. So perhaps Geraldine also was involved in that business. But she wasn't that sort of girl. How do you know, Bryce, he asked himself. Well, let's say she doesn't seem like that sort of girl. Maybe she just happens to know Claude Bernard and the beige man, and they were all having a friendly drink. But there were no glasses in evidence, and neither man had removed his coat. And then Claude in the studio this morning—full of excitement, hatching something. If Claude was edging into the Cloche affair, he'd better look out. Not too sharp, that boy. Tomorrow morning he would pay him a visit, Henry decided. Bernard might heed a warning.

A gentle snore from Louis brought him back to the play.

Egbert dressed himself in his mother's clothes and shot himself, but the shot only went through his leg, which his brother said was just like Egbert he never could do anything properly. The worst of it was the dress was one his mother had planned to wear to a bridge luncheon and she didn't like to after that, she had a funny feeling.

"He really wanted to shoot his mother," Marie whispered to Emily. "The Baroness explained that part to me. He dressed like her so he felt he was shooting her."

"I can't stand psychology." Emily retrieved the hamburger bag from the floor under her seat and found another pickle in it.

When they came out of the theater the snow had turned to rain. Emily was starved. They went to Schrafft's where she had crab salad, and Marie warned her about staying awake all night.

"It's only part of the Human Condition," she sighed. "I wonder if there's a Dog Condition and an Elephant Condition."

"What I want to know is, where were you while we were eating dinner?"

They described the chase, and Louis said, "So it was the man in the camel's hair coat that we saw in Geraldine's apartment?"

"Of course," Henry agreed.

EIGHT

When Emily and Henry got out of the taxi in front of their apartment building, a Mercedes stood at the curb.

"Bernard again," Henry muttered. "I wish he'd park where he belongs, instead of blocking our entrance."

"He'll get a ticket anyway," Emily predicted, walking close to the Mercedes and bracing herself on it before crossing the puddles to the doorway. In the elevator Henry was busy with the keys, and Emily began taking off such items as earrings, belt, bracelets, and the corsage Link had sent to console her for what he correctly foresaw as a trying evening. She unfastened her back garters.

"If you go any further, I'll take out my bridgework," Henry threatened.

He turned on the light in the foyer, and Emily, shedding as she went, trailed into the bedroom. Henry looked across the yards to Geraldine's window. It was dark. So was the one opposite, where they had seen the man in the sheet.

"Henry!" Emily shrieked.

He moved to the bedroom door.

She was sitting on the bed, holding up one of her shoes. "It's bloody!"

"How could it be?"

"How do I know? Look at my hands! Look at the rug!"

From the door to the bed, across the woolly white rug, was a trail of small dark blobs.

"You must have stepped in something," he said.

"It's blood. Can't you see it's blood?"

Henry took the shoe to the light. It could be blood, but he wasn't sure. Without saying anything he traced the footprints back to the foyer, gathered his coat, went down the hall to the elevator, where he pushed the button. He turned to find Emily behind him in a slip, the mink stole, and stocking feet. "Modesty aside," he remarked, "it's cool outside."

"Are you going outside?"

"If the footprints lead that far. Maybe there was a pool of blood in the elevator which we failed to notice."

The elevator floor had the same sticky footprints. Down in the lobby, they led to the door. Outside Henry couldn't see them on the dark pavement, but he could see an oval puddle beside the Mercedes. He walked toward it slowly. Emily took his arm, shivering, and they stood looking down at the stuff, neither one wanting to touch it.

"Open the car door," she said finally. "You know that's where it's coming from."

"I don't know any such thing." Henry peered into the car. The seat was empty but there was a man lying on the floor. He did not look very much alive.

The man was face down with his head toward the curb side of the car. When Henry opened the door a soft white hand slid out and dangled limply. Between the shoulder blades the black wooden handle of a long kitchen knife stuck straight up.

"It's Claude Bernard, isn't it?" Emily whispered.

"I think so. But I don't want to touch him. You go in and call the police from the super's phone."

Emily did not move. "I don't want to go back in there alone, Henry. How do you know the killer isn't hiding in our lobby?"

The lobby was well lighted and very small, but this was no time for argument. He went inside with her and rang the superintendent's bell. Markowitz was not pleased at being called away from a Sherlock Holmes picture.

"I want to call the police," Henry told him. "There's a man lying in a car outside. He looks dead."

"Help yourself." Markowitz waved toward the phone.

Mrs. Markowitz came out of the bedroom and Emily took her outside to show her the blood and the body. Markowitz settled back on his taupe upholstery and went on with Dr. Watson.

Burgreen did not come, and Emily was indignant.

"He has to sleep, even as you and I," Henry pointed out.

The two officers seemed more puzzled by Emily's costume than by the presence of a corpse in the Mercedes. Perhaps corpses were more regular. She explained about the footprints in blood, and their haste to track them down.

After that, she went upstairs, but Henry lingered in the lobby. They were just putting Claude Bernard in the wagon when Link made his way through the small crowd that even at that late hour had somehow got the word and gathered.

"How did you know?" Henry asked.

"Emily phoned me. She says she walked in Bernard's blood. What do you make of this?"

Henry didn't know what he made of it. "I told Claude about the man in the sheet who was watching our windows. You don't suppose he went over there to snoop and got killed?"

"You snooped and they didn't kill you."

"Maybe he ran into something."

Link said it was a little cool to stand outside and think, and they went around the corner to Joe Lacy's.

"Claude must have run onto something," Henry decided.

"I can't imagine Bernard getting very close to murder. He'd faint at the sight of a dead canary."

"You know that girl we call Geraldine, in the apartment on the Park Avenue side of our block? Bernard was in her apartment tonight."

"A girl friend? Claude?"

"I don't think that was it. Because at the same time my man in the camel's hair coat was also there. We followed him when he came out, chased him all over Long Island City and back to Thirty-eighth Street to a grubby little building where he let himself in with a key. He might be living in there—camping. Or maybe he has something hidden there."

"Oh, sure. The papers."

Henry, gazing at a sign that had electric beer running out of a tap, went on thinking about the man. "If I knew who he was, I might have a start. He's definitely interested in the Cloche affair, and now it looks as if he knew Claude Bernard."

Link put down his glass. "Bernard must have been on the track of some money—that was his number one problem. Since he suddenly ceased to be, one might guess that his approach was blackmail."

"But who was he blackmailing? Geraldine lives a puritanical life. At least while the shades are up."

"Your man in the camel's hair coat. The question is, was he someone Bernard already knew? Was he a friend? Or a business acquaintance?"

Henry felt sure the man in the camel's hair coat was not a decorator.

"He still might be a friend," Link observed. "The man who knows most about Claude and Claude's troubles is Mr. Boomer. We couldn't call old Boomer this time of night, could we?"

"Certainly not," Henry agreed, and went to the pay phone on the wall.

"What the hell do you want?" Boomer demanded. "Do you know what time it is? Can't a man have any peace in this goddamned town?"

"Hello, Gus," Henry said amiably. "Just thought you might be lonesome, being a widower and all. Link Simpson and I are down at Joe Lacy's having one. Why don't you hop a cab and come over?"

Boomer was for once speechless, but only for a second. "Do you know what time I get up in the morning? I've got an appointment at seven-thirty, you bastard."

"Gus, listen to me. Bernard was stabbed in his car in front of our building tonight. Emily and I found him."

"Yeah?" The tone changed. "So he didn't have to slash his wrists. My God, this is getting rough on the decorating business, Bryce. How are you feeling?"

"So far, only curious. Link and I were chewing it over, and we decided you knew more about Claude Bernard than anybody. Is he mixed up with a fellow who always wears a camel's hair coat?"

"Only fellow he's mixed up with that I know is Hazen Armstrong, and he's out of the country."

"What does he look like?"

"Look like? God, I don't know. I'm no student of human nature. I just try to get what's coming to my clients."

"Surely you have some idea … Is he tall or short, dark or light, fat or thin?"

"Kind of neutral," Boomer reflected.

"Did he wear a camel's hair topcoat?"

"The times we had our summit meetings it was a hundred and one in the shade of Chase Manhattan."

"Is he the type that would wear a camel's hair topcoat?"

"There you go again—philosophy, psychology. I don't know what type of man wears what type of coat. Whatever a man can afford, he wears. Don't he?"

"Are you still trying to collect from him?"

"He's out of the country. Looking after his foreign investments."

"What foreign investments?" Henry wondered.

"That's what I said. 'What foreign investments?' So he gives me a line about tin and copper and zinc."

"No diamonds?"

"Didn't mention 'em. And I don't think it is tin or copper or zinc. It's something quicker than digging it out of the ground."

Henry was a little surprised that Boomer believed there were any foreign investments.

"Maybe I'm a sucker, Bryce. But he was convincing. I never heard a more sincere line, outside of a kidney pill ad."

"Did you talk to his wife?"

"Naturally. One doesn't attack the fort only from one side. She gave me the same stuff about investments, and brother does she have charm. She could sell me an organdy nightshirt with lace insertion."

Henry let Boomer go back to bed, and returned to his stool at the bar. "He has no grasp of the human appearance. Couldn't describe Armstrong at all. It should be easy to find Boomer a wife—anything would do."

The next morning Henry ate his doughnut in silence, glad that Gottlieb was too busy fixing coffee for the Sicilian Paving Company's street drillers to ask questions about the departure of Claude Bernard. Henry was very tired and looked with a liverish eye on anyone threatening to ask a question, even a simple question like which way is Fifth Avenue.

The *Daily News*, with its soporific smell of burning passion, crash of breaking homes, and gurgle of love letters being flushed down the toilet, had failed in its usual job of putting Emily to sleep. She had kept Henry awake with speculation and fantasy about Bernard's death until nearly four o'clock. She was now developing a head cold which she insisted had nothing to do with walking in Sixty-second Street in her stocking feet.

As he came up Second Avenue, Henry saw that Jerry Lauterbach was again having trouble with the neighborhood psycho. It was natural, Henry reflected, that New York, being so well supplied with all the necessities of life, should not be lacking in persons whose mental furniture was sliding about on the polished floors of their intelligence. Jerry usually kept a table and chair in front of his shop, and this young fellow liked to sit there and read Thomas Aquinas. He was the successor to the old man who used to lean into the studio once a day and announce, "This is Abelard. The only flavor left is chocolate. Okay?"

Emily always answered politely, "That's okay, Mr. Abelard," and he would smile and go off. He stopped coming, perhaps not of his own volition, and for a month that part of Second Avenue was deprived of a psycho. The vacancy was then filled by this young reader.

"Damned nuisance," Jerry muttered, as the fellow got up, casting a black look at Henry, and moved away. "Say, what do you know about our friend Bernard? I can't believe it. He seemed too sharp to let himself get murdered. With a butcher knife, too. No style, no class."

"No bullet, no gun, no owner," Henry added.

"Right. I saw Bernard yesterday morning. He came in and looked at some pieces, and I wasn't very friendly, knowing his financial condition, but he hinted that he was about to change all that. He didn't actually say so, but I thought it was some scheme he had to collect from Armstrong. Maybe I imagined that, because I knew that's where he'd gone broke. Actually I didn't pay too much attention, figured he was giving me a line."

"Did he give you any hint as to what the scheme might be?" Henry asked.

Lauterbach shook his head. "Whatever it was, it looks as if somebody found it annoying."

"The only person who might find it embarrassing, I should think, would be Armstrong, who owed the money. And Armstrong isn't here. He's out of the country."

"Who says so?"

"August Boomer."

"August generally has the right dope."

When Henry told Emily about Jerry's idea that Bernard was trying to collect the Armstrong decorating bill, Emily said, "How? By long distance? Henry, call Mr. Burgreen right away.

And put the hardware on the TV cabinet, so we can get out of here before lunch."

Henry disliked the imperative when applied to himself. With more than his usual deliberateness he got into his dungarees. Then he stood at his desk to open the mail.

"Henry, I told you, Mr. Burgreen wants you to call him," Emily pleaded.

"In good time." There was a letter from his aunt in Dutchess County. He read it aloud to Emily, who did not wish to hear it.

> Dear Henry:
>
> If you are the Henry Bryce who has been working on this outrageous solid gold furniture for the UN man who has been murdering women in New York, it is going to be terribly embarrassing for me at the next DAR meeting. You know how they feel about the UN, and now this just proves all these foreigners are only in it for the money and we ought to get them out of that nice building the Rockefellers built and use it for something worthwhile like Girl Scouts.

"Wait till she hears we found Claude's body," Henry remarked. "I wish I could find a photograph of Hazen Armstrong."

"You could go over to *The Times* morgue this afternoon, instead of getting your hair cut at the St. Regis."

"What makes you think they'd have his picture?"

"People like that get into *The Times* when they marry."

"Not men. Only women. Men have to die to get into *The Times*. I'd better call Burgreen." The phone rang, bringing on Marie. He started to tell her about finding Claude's body, but she informed him she had been all over that with Emily. She wanted to know if there was anything new.

"Not much. There's a chance he was trying to get his money out of Armstrong, although Boomer says Armstrong is out of the country. I'd like to get hold of a photograph of that man."

"Louis has a picture of his ribs. He fell downstairs last summer and somebody sent him to Louis, and of course we never collected the bill."

Henry didn't think a picture of Armstrong's ribs would be much help. "Did you get your diamonds back in the bank, Marie?"

"How could I, on Saturday?"

"Have a nice worried weekend." Henry called Louis at his office, asked for a description of Hazen Armstrong. He could hear a drawer open and a chair squeak.

"Here's the card," Louis said. "He's five feet nine, weight one-sixty, age forty-five, blood pressure normal, chronic indigestion. Want the childhood diseases?"

"Hell, no. What did he look like?"

"He had a clear white skin, I remember. Touch of color in the cheeks. Dark eyes, dark hair, little dark mustache."

"It sounds all wrong for my man. What kind of overcoat was he wearing?"

"I generally examine them with their overcoats off. Anyway, it was summer."

"I hear you liked it so much you're seeing *Down the Drain* again tonight."

"I hear you're coming with us. Too bad about Bernard. Do they know anything yet?"

"They're just beginning on it." Henry hung up.

The phone rang again. "Where have you been?" Burgreen demanded. "Do you know anything about Bernard that you didn't tell the boys last night?"

"We saw him in an apartment on the Park Avenue side of our block, about seven o'clock."

"Whose apartment?"

"We don't know. We call her Geraldine. First time we've ever seen a man there, and this time there were two. The other one was the man in the camel's hair coat."

Burgreen didn't say anything for a moment. "You're pretty

much attached to this fellow in the camel's hair coat, aren't you, Bryce?"

"He does have a way of turning up before, during, and after." Henry told him about seeing the beige man enter the deserted beauty shop on Thirty-eighth Street last night.

Burgreen did not show any great interest. What he wanted now was the location of Geraldine's apartment. Henry gave it to him. "What do you know about this girl whose name is probably not Geraldine?" he demanded.

Very little, Henry said, except that she was a person of efficient and fixed habits. She had dinner at a certain hour, sat in a certain chair to eat it, read *The Wall Street Journal* while she ate. "I've never heard her voice, but I'd bet she has a commanding baritone. Not easy to get along with, unless you do all the giving in. Sort of on the order of Mrs. Lorenz."

"You've never seen Bernard in her apartment before?"

"No."

Burgreen said he would explore the possibility that Geraldine was Bernard's girl friend.

Henry turned to Emily. "Burgreen says maybe Geraldine was Claude's girl friend."

Emily said Claude thought girls were something you added to a room for interest—like a potted plant.

"Do you think this murder is tied in any way to the other one?" Henry asked Burgreen.

"I have no theories yet. Trying to get a picture of Bernard. I'm in his apartment right now. He liked Chopin and dark green and he could have parked a freight truck on his bed. Probably reluctant to give up all this plush. Might have been working on ways to avoid giving it up. Maybe he had a helpful piece of information that he offered to Pierre Cloche, at a price."

"Why would Cloche kill him for trying to be helpful?"

Emily interrupted. "Where is he?" Henry told her. "Tell him we're coming over to help him. We can show him where Geraldine lives."

"What about all this work you were determined to finish?"

"Nobody works on Saturday, Henry."

He gave Burgreen the news, and if the detective didn't sound exactly overjoyed, neither did he order them not to come.

Burgreen was looking through Bernard's checkbook when they entered the elegant dark-green living room.

"Jerry Lauterbach thinks Bernard was working on some scheme to get his money out of Armstrong," Henry announced.

"Is that so? And who is Jerry Lauterbach?"

Henry told him, and Burgreen's expression did not indicate any confidence in the opinions of Mr. Lauterbach.

"I thought myself Bernard was up to something yesterday." Henry admitted, not liking to have things brushed off this way. "He was sort of walking on his toes—ready to take off into the upper air."

Burgreen said since when did the way a man walked indicate that he was about to rejuvenate his bank account?

Emily disappeared into the bedroom. In a moment she came out wearing a huge leghorn hat, vintage 1900, somewhat battered. "Isn't it stunning?" she demanded.

"I saw that in the wastebasket in there," Burgreen remarked. "I wonder what he was doing with it?"

"Throwing it away. I think I'll keep it."

"You will not," Henry said firmly. "Put it back where you found it."

"It's still perfectly good, if you had it blocked. I can see a gorgeous pink rose on one side, can't you, Mr. Burgreen?"

"Put it back," Henry begged. "You've gotten all the audience reaction you're entitled to."

"Maybe an ostrich plume?" Emily tossed the hat on a couch and swung back a pair of jalousies, revealing the kitchen. She opened the refrigerator. "He didn't expect to be murdered. Not right away, at least. Two big steaks and frozen french fries and broccoli and cheesecake. It seems a shame to let all this good food go to waste."

3

"Those steaks belong to the heirs," Henry warned.

"Who are Claude's heirs?"

Burgreen said no will had turned up. He began replacing the papers in the desk and straightening things out. Burgreen was a very orderly type.

There were sounds of rattling paper, opening and closing drawers and clanking cutlery. Emily had found a loaf of Italian bread and a roll of salami and was making sandwiches.

"I'd like a cup of green tea," Burgreen admitted. "Don't suppose he had any."

He had, and presently they were scattering crumbs on Claude's cream-colored carpet and his antique glass coffee table.

Burgreen looked around the room. "You know, I don't see why a man with such fastidious taste, so orderly in all his housekeeping, would have a dirty face."

They both looked at him, puzzled.

"His face was lying on the floor of the car, Mr. Burgreen," Emily reminded him.

"Not that kind of dirt. Not dust. There was a dirty line at the edge of his hair."

"A dye job?"

"No, nothing like that. I don't know what it was, and the report hasn't come in yet."

Something—some connection with another event—started to form in Henry's mind, and then dissolved because Burgreen suddenly set down his teacup.

"I've got to be on my way. Meeting my wife for a little Christmas shopping."

"You're not going to Geraldine's?" Emily cried.

"No great urgency there."

"Mr. Burgreen, you are going there and you just don't want us along."

The detective smiled. "That was the general idea."

"I won't get in the way. Really."

He shrugged. "Irregular, but if you feel you must—"

Emily gathered up the dishes—a symptom which Henry should have regarded with suspicion but he was thinking of other things—and they left Claude's apartment.

NINE

The doorman guarding Geraldine's building was at the moment
of their arrival suffering from gastritis. He was inclined to take
a dismal view of his own species, and wanted to be left alone.
He came most reluctantly to the conclusion that Burgreen actually was a police officer, although accompanied by two civilian
persons, one of whom carried a brown paper sack under a sec-
ond-rate mink stole. Burgreen worked out of him the information that the occupant of the third floor rear apartment was Miss
Geraldine Seabrook.

Burgreen turned on Henry. "I thought you didn't know her?"

"We don't."

"But you knew her first name."

Emily explained they had only happened to guess her real
name. Burgreen looked skeptical.

Henry noticed the grocery bag in Emily's arm. "What did
you steal from poor Claude?" he demanded, while they waited
for the doorman to ring Miss Seabrook.

"Steal?" Emily gave him a wide innocent stare. "Henry, this
is my knitting."

"You haven't knitted anything since the Boer War."

Miss Seabrook did not answer her phone.

"Have you seen her today?" Burgreen asked the doorman.

"No."

"When did you come on duty?"

"Eight this morning."

"I think we'd better take a look at her apartment."

"You don't think something's happened to her?"

"I don't know. We'd better see."

They crowded into the small gilt elevator, and rose to the third floor. "I don't think I'll go in with you," Emily decided. "You look and tell me."

The doorman turned the key gingerly, as if he feared a gas explosion, and Henry followed Burgreen through the dark foyer into the austere room they could see from their own apartment. The bamboo shade was still down, and heavy brown draperies were drawn across it. Burgreen switched on lights, peered into the bathroom and the bedroom, swung open the doors hiding a compact shining kitchenette. There was no one in the rooms. "No bodies," he told Emily. Against a wall was a filing cabinet, empty. Miss Seabrook's bedroom closet was not empty, but it contained a dozen or so bare hangers, scattered among the dresses and skirts and blouses still there.

"No luggage anywhere. Clothes missing."

Emily looked into the closet. "Her embroidered housecoat is still here. She wouldn't go willingly without that."

Emily made an inspection of the bathroom, remarking on the ferocious color of the shower curtain.

There was another closet in the foyer, containing several coats, an umbrella and snow boots.

"She's gone to Florida, if not to heaven," Emily concluded.

"What makes you think so?" The voice was quiet and scornful.

Henry turned to see Geraldine in the doorway.

"Miss Seabrook!" The doorman's tone was so respectful as to suggest a genuflection. "This man is a policeman and he had me open up to see if you were all right."

"And what made the policeman think I might not be all right?"

Burgreen took Miss Seabrook calmly. He was not fond of the

executive type, Henry suspected, but he made an effort to be friendly. He said he understood she knew Mr. Claude Bernard, who had met with an unfortunate accident last night.

"I've never heard of him," she said.

"He'd be hurt," Emily told her. "He thought he was the most important decorator north of Bloomingdale's."

"I have no contact with decorators," Miss Seabrook explained. "Who told you I knew Mr. Bernard?"

Burgreen ignored that. "You use your apartment as an office, Miss Seabrook?"

"I used to. I don't any longer."

"By any longer, do you mean since last night?"

"I really will have to know why you are questioning me, and I think I ought to consult my lawyer."

Burgreen tried a couple of other questions—what line of business was she in, and did she work for someone else? She refused to answer.

"That's all right," he said easily. "We'll be meeting again, no doubt. Meanwhile, if anything should occur to you that might throw light on Mr. Bernard's murder, call me at this number." He scribbled it for her.

Either she had extremely good control, or she already knew that Claude had been murdered. She asked no questions about how or where he had met his death. "Since I've never seen Mr. Bernard," she said firmly, "it seems unlikely that anything would occur to me." She accepted the note all the same, and placed it under a small brass cat on the desk. She also lined up the onyx pen holder, the brown blotter with leather edges, the heavy crystal ash tray and the square-based bronze lamp. It occurred to Henry that she must have left the apartment in a hurry, or these things would not have been out of alignment with the edge of the desk. The girl was a fiend for order.

The doorman stayed to square himself with Miss Seabrook, and in the elevator going down Burgreen conceded that perhaps something interesting had been going on here.

"Unless, of course, you were mistaken about Claude Bernard

in her apartment last night. It's quite a distance to make a positive identification."

"You come up to our place and we'll show you how well you can see with those glasses."

Burgreen said no thanks, he had to get to Macy's to begin suffering in honor of the Christmas spirit.

"Do you think it would be worthwhile to check the address on Thirty-eighth Street?" Henry asked.

"What address? … Oh, your camel's hair man." Burgreen wrote down the location and said he'd send a man to have a look. He didn't say when. As they paused in the street before parting, he added soberly, "If you want to spend Christmas together, keep away from Miss Seabrook."

"Do you think she's dangerous?" Emily asked.

"Anybody connected with murder is dangerous. She may be connected. Until we know, let's quarantine her. Enjoy the steaks, Mrs. Bryce."

Emily gave him a startled smile, hugged the brown paper bag under her stole. It seemed to Henry that the bag was somewhat bulkier than it had been when they entered the building.

"He's right, too," Emily said thoughtfully as she and Henry turned the corner into Sixty-second Street. "She had a funny look when he mentioned Claude. I wonder if that man in the overcoat told her we followed him last night? He probably did."

Henry left her at the door of their building, but instead of going to the St. Regis for his haircut he made for Quentin Hill's bookshop. Mr. Hill, a large hollow-chested man with a gray face, was sorting flower prints.

"Too bad about poor Bernard, wasn't it?" Henry began.

"Hell of a thing. Butcher knife, they say. Is that right? I heard you found him."

"We did. And it was a butcher knife."

"One of these savages from Harlem, I suppose."

"More inclined to use a switch-blade knife," Henry suggested. "Who has the rear apartment on the third floor in this building?"

"That one's empty. That's where the French hair dresser lived. Why?"

Henry saw no reason why he shouldn't tell Hill that someone had seemed to be watching their windows from that apartment on Thursday night.

Hill looked skeptical. "How do you know he was watching you, Bryce? I should think that would be very difficult to be sure of."

"We may have been mistaken. Anyway, we didn't see him last night. But we saw Claude in a lady's apartment. Do you know a gal named Geraldine Seabrook?"

Hill said he did not. "You seem to be quite active with your spying, Bryce," he added sharply.

"It's a harmless pastime for Mrs. Bryce. She seems to like to know what other people are having for dinner."

"This goes beyond broiled chicken. I shall be very careful in future to pull my curtains after dark."

"Where is your apartment?" Henry asked, smiling.

"Ground floor rear."

"You and Bernard were friends, weren't you?" Hill nodded. "Did he ever mention a Miss Seabrook?"

"No. Where did she live?"

"Third floor rear of a building in the middle of the block on the Park Avenue side." Henry was startled to see the effect of this information on Hill. Up to this point he appeared saddened by the fate of his friend, interested, curious, but nothing more. Now, just for a moment, before he dropped those sheltering white eyelids over his wary eyes, he betrayed a stronger emotion. Whether it was shock or fright, Henry couldn't tell.

"Who else was in the apartment?" Hill asked, turning over one of the flower prints.

"A man in a camel's hair coat—don't know who he is."

"No one else?"

"Only Miss Seabrook. There could have been someone else, not visible from our windows." Henry didn't know whether this statement relieved Hill or not.

"Are you sure this person you saw in my building wasn't watching Miss Seabrook's apartment rather than yours?"

That was an interesting possibility, Henry admitted. "Anyway, he didn't want to be identified."

"How do you know?"

"As I stepped into the apartment he grabbed me around the ankles, threw me, and ran like hell."

Hill was surprised. "Were you in that apartment? When did this take place?"

"Night before last. I came over to investigate. The door was unlocked, so I walked in."

"That was bright. You might have been killed."

Henry agreed. "I thought I was being cautious when I threw the door wide open before I went in. But he didn't come from behind the door."

Hill didn't like the idea of strange people, perhaps murderers, invading his building. "I don't see how he got a key, Bryce. Nobody had a key to that apartment but me, and I'm not spending my evenings watching people in other dwellings around the block."

"You're too tall for our man in the gold turban," Henry assured him.

"Let's go up and see if that door is still unlocked." Hill took a bunch of keys from a desk drawer, and they went upstairs.

The door was still unlocked, and the sheet was still on the closet floor with the gold turban and the feathers with the fake emeralds. Henry went to the windows. It was quite easy to see Miss Seabrook's apartment from here. He pointed it out to Hill. "Perhaps you're right and he was watching over there, to see if Bernard would appear."

"You mean," Hill gathered his words deliberately, "that this fellow who used my premises for spying is Bernard's murderer?"

Henry said he could be.

"I don't follow you."

"There are some large gaps," Henry admitted. "All we know is that he was spying on somebody, and there's no percentage in watching the Bryces."

Hill said dryly there were a great many other windows visible from here, and a man might have other reasons than murder for watching someone.

"He was very anxious not to be seen and recognized," Henry argued. "Look at this crazy disguise."

"There's at least one person in every block crazy enough to dress like that, just for his own amusement. Or to scare people." He picked up the gold turban, examined it. "Very neat sewing job. Does it seem likely a man with such imagination would employ a butcher knife for a killing?"

"He wasn't terribly neat. Look at the basin in the bathroom."

Hill went in there and ran his finger around the basin. "Greasy," he remarked.

"Could your last tenant have left it that way?"

"Certainly not—I had the place cleaned."

"I wonder why he went to so much trouble?"

Hill smiled. "He was afraid of Mrs. Bryce's powerful glass."

In that case, Henry observed as he and Hill went down the stairs, he was someone who knew them, knew that Emily used the binoculars.

Henry left Quentin Hill looking somewhat disturbed and started for the St. Regis. Then he thought he would drop in and tell Link they had finally met Geraldine.

Link was busy with a South American millionaire who collected Nazi regalia, and two other men were looking at a Sharps rifle. Link's shop was crowded with nobody in it, and with three customers motion became impossible. He had a boy who helped him, and this boy was expert at getting through invisible cracks between people and artillery. He was also a genius at finding a particular weapon in the incredible confusion of drawers, shelves, walls, bins, and a basement all crammed with guns, swords, daggers, helmets, chain mail, and spears.

"Wheeler was just in," Link said in a quick aside. "He was pretty much shaken by Bernard's death."

Henry raised a questioning eyebrow, squeezed himself against a wooden horse in a suit of armor so that the two men could get past him and work their way out of the place.

"Seemed to think this one was connected with Camilla."

"Did he say why?"

Link shook his head.

The South American demanded Link's attention. Henry leaned on the horse and tried to think. The straw hat in Claude's wastebasket floated through his head, and after it the inevitable man in the camel's hair coat. It annoyed him that Burgreen refused to take that character seriously. He knew Burgreen wasn't going to send a man down to Thirty-eighth Street today—too busy getting to Macy's on time, and once he got into Macy's he would have to concentrate on survival.

Link was finally closing the deal—the gentleman was writing a check. With a restricted flourish of his walking stick and a smell of good cigar, he was gone.

"Can you think of any reason in the world why Claude would have a lady's straw hat, vintage about 1900, in his wastebasket?" Henry asked.

"No." Link put away the boxes of stuff he had been showing. "Anything else?"

"A couple of steaks which Emily stole. Come and have dinner?"

"I'd like to, but there's a girl who will go hungry if I do. This wouldn't matter, if she were not the owner of a large and empty barn over in Jersey. I can't afford to disappoint a lady who can easily store a dozen cannons for an indefinite time at practically no cost."

"I think I'll go down to Thirty-eighth Street right now and have a look in May's Salon de Beauté. If you don't hear from me in three or four weeks, send a cop."

Link looked concerned. "I don't like that idea, Bryce. Wait

till five, and I'll go with you."

"Nothing will happen to me—I'm easily frightened."

"Does Emily know you're going?"

"No. And don't you tell her. Think about that straw hat, will you? By the way, Quentin Hill thinks the man in the sheet was probably not watching us at all—maybe he had his eyes on Geraldine's place. Maybe he saw Claude there and then put an end to him."

"Just for being in Geraldine's apartment? Drastic."

"Let it be a lesson to you, my boy."

It was snowing hard when Henry paid the cab driver at the corner of Thirty-eighth Street and Second Avenue and walked toward May's Beauty Salon. The street was empty, the snow drifting into gritty doorways and blowing across stained window panes. A man in a gray undershirt stood picking his lunch out of his teeth at one of the windows. Otherwise the whole block might have been uninhabited.

He approached the curtained shop front slowly, walked past to see if there were a light inside. There was none. He came back and knocked. There was no response, but he hadn't expected any. The door was locked. He looked across the street to see if he were observed. The building opposite was boarded up, and no one appeared at any of the windows on either side of it. He gave the door a good shove with his shoulder. The lock rattled loosely, but it held. He took a penknife from his pocket, slid it into the wide crack between the door and frame, shoved the catch back. After another quick glance up and down the street, he entered the dim room, closed the door after him, and stood motionless, listening.

The place was cold and smelled of tobacco, old wallpaper, dust—everything but the strong perfumes of hair manipulation. It must have been a long time since May had worked here. The pale light seeped over two dryers, a cracked washbasin, a shelf with a few bottles, a plastic hairbrush, and some wire rollers. A door on the inside wall stood slightly ajar. He crossed the room, his shoes crunching the grit on the cracked linoleum, and opened the door. It led to a dark hall and a stairway. He could hear no sound of life, but on the worn linoleum near another door on the left, he saw two glistening small puddles. Someone with wet shoes had recently walked on this floor. It would be foolhardy to go on down the hall and open that door. Nevertheless he did go on, and cautiously swung open the door. The room inside was almost dark, and had an embalmed smell of cooking.

When he found a light switch he saw a dirty gas range, an iron sink, a gas heater, and a narrow cot with no springs. On this cot were an air mattress, a pair of pale blue percale sheets—not very clean—a fine white wool blanket and a pale blue silk comforter embroidered with pink flowers. The pillow was soft and plump and encased in the same blue percale. Under the pillow was a paperbound copy of a novel in what Henry thought was French.

Someone had spent some uncomfortable hours here, waiting and reading. The broiler pan in the stove looked as if it had passed through sessions without a wash. The occupant of the enchanting premises had apparently eaten from a frozen-dinner aluminum plate, and drunk from a jelly glass. There were chop bones in a paper bag on the splintered wooden drainboard. There was something else in the paper bag—an almost empty pink glass bottle labeled YOUNG AND FAIR. After perusing the label and applying a little of the sticky liquid to his wrist, Henry concluded it was a form of makeup. So perhaps the occupant of the bed was a woman? He went over and looked closely at the top sheet and the pillowslip. Not a single lipstick stain. Neither did the garbage bag contain any tissues with lipstick marks. Unlikely that a woman who used liquid makeup would omit lipstick.

But why would a man be using makeup? He studied the color on his wrist. A sort of neutral tone—not suntan and not blond. Honey colored? Beige? Of course beige! His beige man in the overcoat was not really that color, he was covering his complexion.

He ought to report all this to Burgreen, but Burgreen was in Macy's. Anyway, he could take the bottle for possible fingerprints. He started toward the sink, halted. Had he heard the stairs creak? He held his breath, but no further sound came from the hall. He'd better get out of here. He dropped the makeup bottle in his coat pocket and went quickly down the hall to the beauty shop, crossed to the street door and would have gone safely through it, if he hadn't noticed what seemed to be a pile of dirty cretonne curtains near the basin. Something made him lift the cretonne. Under it, stacked against the wall, were a number of bulging file folders. He closed the hall door and picked up the top folder, opened it, read the heading on the first letter:

The Royal Development Company CELESTIA GAAD

His eyes ran hungrily down the page, and he did not hear the hall door at his back open. He was aware suddenly of a rush of cold air on his neck. Still clutching the folder, he stepped hastily to the outside door, put his left hand on the worn brass knob. He did not open the door.

TEN

Henry felt terribly cold. The electric blanket must have failed again. There was a draft on his head, too.

"Emily, close the window, will you?" he groaned.

There was no response and the draft seemed to have snow in it. He opened his eyes. He was lying on concrete, lightly padded with snow. It was dark, but the light coming through the green glass windows of an ancient liquor dispensary fell on a brace of garbage cans in front of him.

Feet, two pairs, female, came clicking toward him.

"Don't you hate to see a man in that condition?"

"His poor wife is probably home waiting dinner for him."

"If she is, it's the first time since we've been married," Henry muttered, watching the feet disappear.

He was trying to get up when a slower pair of feet came along, accompanied by a cane. "And is it a comfort to you to be lying on the cold snow of a winter's night, young man?" The voice was kindly, curious, only faintly chiding.

"It is not," Henry answered. "Could you help me get to the door of this place?"

"Is it the doctor's office you'd be wanting then? I think it could be managed." The cane dropped to the walk, a strong pair of hands gripped Henry under the arms, and he got shakily to his feet.

Another fellow came along. "And what's this you're doing, Mr. Casey? Is the poor man under the influence?"

"He's in need of a bit of medicine, John, that's plain. Help me to get him into Gallagher's."

"But he's already had too much. You're not doing him a kindness to take him back into Gallagher's when it's plain it's from Gallagher's he's been thrown out."

"I was not thrown out," Henry protested. "All I want is one short drink, so I can get home to my poor starving wife and my seven little children."

"You'd best be going home without that little drop," John advised.

"Now, John, what harm can one more drink do a man in his condition? Give me your help, not your pious reflections."

John succumbed, and the two of them ushered Henry into Gallagher's. An embarrassing possibility occurred to him as they sat him on a stool and took places on either side of him. Perhaps he had been robbed. His hand found the reassuring bulge of his wallet, and inspection showed a twenty-dollar bill and a couple of ones. He invited his friends to join him, and they had three. Henry's strength returned, to the immense satisfaction of his first benefactor, and the surprise of the second.

"You know, I don't believe he was drunk," John remarked.

"I wasn't. Someone in May's Beauty Salon slugged me."

"May's Beauty Salon." They looked mystified. "The place is vacant—it's been vacant for months—years. What were you doing in there?"

"Looking for a man in a camel's hair coat."

John winked across Henry at Mr. Casey. "His trouble's not drink. A bit mental."

"It's a long story," Henry explained. "If I went back now, perhaps I could get some of the letters."

"He's a spy, Mr. Casey. He's after the papers."

"Would these be hydrogen or uranium papers, sir?"

Henry smiled. "Come with me and I'll show you."

John thought it was much warmer and cheerier in Gallagher's than it could possibly be in May's Beauty Salon. Mr. Casey, however, had the spirit of adventure. He took his cane from the bar, prodded John off his stool, and the three got as far as the door, when John halted. "Why don't you tell us first, over a nice glass of something, why you must have these papers, Mr. Bryce?"

"I would, but for my poor wife waiting for me at home," Henry said earnestly. "I'll tell you about it on the way down the street." He did so, briefly, and both his friends shook their heads and pronounced that Old England was at the bottom of the whole thing.

"Wherever there's a bit of treachery, a puddle of blood, the bread snatched from the mouth of the orphan, you'll find Old England has her dirty hands in it," John said.

They reached May's, and found the place quite dark. The door was locked, and Henry repeated his work with the pen-knife. Even flanked by these good friends he had a distinctly tight feeling in his chest and throat as he groped for the light button on the wall. There was no need for apprehension. The file folders were gone, every one of them. Not a letter, not a scrap of paper remained.

Mr. Casey gave him an embarrassed smile, full of pity for his mental state.

"They must have moved the stuff as soon as they got rid of me," Henry said.

"Sure. Sure, that's it," John agreed. "Now you'd best get home to your wife, poor woman."

They put him tenderly into a cab, and said goodbye.

Henry gave the driver his own address, suddenly changed his mind, and went to Beekman Place. He didn't know exactly what he was going to do when he reached the Armstrong apartment, but he combed his hair, wiped his face with a handkerchief, and hoped he didn't look too wrinkled.

The doorman told him Mr. Armstrong was out of the country

and his apartment had been sublet to a Mrs. Christie. Henry said he was an old school friend who wanted to locate Hazen, and perhaps Mrs. Christie could help him.

The doorman didn't think so, but he rang her and Henry got permission to go up. Mrs. Christie let him in somewhat reluctantly. The apartment was gorgeously unfurnished—French wallpaper, brocade draperies, deep carpet—and Mrs. Christie had tried to patch the gaps left by the reclaimed pieces but neither her taste nor her purse was equal to the job.

"If you're another creditor, you're wasting your time," she told him. "I don't know where he is, and I don't know where his wife is. I pay the agent, and have no contact with the Armstrongs."

"I'm not a creditor," Henry said. "Perhaps you don't know that the decorator who did this apartment was murdered last night."

"No, I didn't know that." She looked frightened.

"I'm not a detective, or anybody official, and you don't have to talk to me at all, Mrs. Christie." He put on his warmest smile and looked humble.

"Who are you, then, Mr. Bryce?"

He explained, added that he didn't necessarily think Armstrong had killed Mr. Bernard, but he did suspect Armstrong might be in New York, and might be involved. If only he knew what the man looked like—was there a photograph of him in the apartment?

She hadn't seen one, but there were things in drawers that she hadn't looked through, naturally.

While they stood there talking, Henry noticed on the wall behind Mrs. Christie a fair water color of a stretch of river. "Yours?" he asked.

"No. Something Mr. Armstrong did—there are several." Henry stepped closer, "The Maas, H.A.," he read. "Where is the Maas?" Mrs. Christie didn't know. He called the public library, which was tired but dredged up the information that the

Maas was also the Meuse of Belgium.

"Whipped cream!" he cried, and shook Mrs. Christie's hand. "Thank you very much. Goodbye."

"I don't understand," she pleaded, but Henry was halfway to the elevator.

As Henry put the key in the lock of his apartment, he was ready for a blast of questions and accusations from Emily. The apartment was dark. When he lighted it he found confusion. Someone had emptied all the drawers in the place, and there were socks, shorts, slips, bathtowels, sheets, table mats, and silver on the floor. Nothing was damaged, but everything had been moved. In the foyer closet three coats had dropped from their hangers. Even the kitchen had been ransacked—the drawer in the stove, containing pots and pans, and the glass door of the rotisserie stood open.

Where was Emily? Panic started to rise in him, his heart hammered. Easy, he told himself. Nothing's happened to Emily. They could search the place without hurting her. She probably wasn't even here when they came. But where was she now? She generally cleaned on Saturday. The only evidence of a start in that direction was the hose of the vacuum cleaner, lying in front of the bathroom door, and the box of tree ornaments on the coffee table. He sat down and opened the box, wondering why people called it a coffee table—why not an ashes and whiskey and old newspapers table? He lifted out a couple of yards of tinsel, a pink frosted glass ball, and a red flannel Santa Claus dear to Emily's heart. It had graced their first tree and they were never to part with it. The sight of this grimy and frayed little man made him feel a sharper twinge about Emily.

Perhaps she'd got tired waiting for him to come home to get dinner and had gone over to the Barbizon for a bite. Or maybe Link had invited her out. He called Link, but Link hadn't heard from Emily. He was getting ready to take the girl from New Jersey to dinner.

"The whole place here has been searched. God knows what

they were looking for or what they've done with Emily."

"Take it easy, Emily's all right."

"I hope she is. But where is she?"

"Call Marie before you call the morgue. Your place has been subjected to the usual robbery, that's all."

"With silver lying all over the floor? It's something to do with the murders."

"I'd better call off my date and come over."

"No—just tell me where you're going to be."

"Leo's for dinner. After that"—Link paused—"if all goes well, we'll be here."

"Okay. Fine."

"Sure you don't want me to come over?"

"No, thanks. Get off the line so I can call Marie."

Marie was keenly interested. She had no information on Emily's whereabouts. "I can see her lying in some empty lot with a knife in her back," she said.

"Stop trying to cheer me up."

"What are you going to do, Henry?"

"Call the police."

"It's probably too late for that. But go ahead."

He dropped the phone, hoping it would hurt her ear, and got the 17th Precinct. They were reluctant to give him Burgreen's home number, but he said he had some urgent new evidence he was sure Burgreen would want. When Burgreen answered from his home on Staten Island, he didn't sound as if he cared about new evidence. Three hours in Macy's had undone him.

"Emily's disappeared." Henry tried to sound matter-of-fact. "Our apartment has been thoroughly searched. May's Beauty Salon was loaded with correspondence from the Royal Development Company of Gaad."

Burgreen suddenly dropped the contemplation of his aching feet. "Did you secure some of this correspondence?"

"Tried to. Somebody caught me at it, and rendered me unconscious."

"How long ago was this?"

"I went down there about an hour after I left you. Didn't come to in front of Gallagher's saloon until after dark."

"Oh, God. I'll get a car down there right away."

"No hurry. The files are all gone. I went back to see, with two strong companions."

Burgreen controlled himself. "That's what happens when you amateurs wade into a case—everything gets lost, all the principals are warned in plenty of time, and the evidence vanishes."

"I'm sorry," Henry said, "but remember who found May's Beauty Salon."

"That was fine. That was good work. But why can't you fellows let your good work alone after you've done it? Did you read any of the letters?"

Henry admitted that he hadn't had time.

"Someone's been sleeping in the building—in a room at the back. Blue percale sheets. A novel in French. And an empty bottle of liquid makeup, more or less beige in color. What do you make of that?"

"Your beige man is a woman."

"No lipstick. A woman who used liquid makeup would use lipstick, wouldn't she? I think it's a man who wants to cover a ruddy complexion, or freckles or something. Maybe even a scar."

Burgreen was interested. "I don't believe that stuff would cover a scar. I think your idea about complexion is closer."

"Also, I found out that Hazen Armstrong spent some time in Belgium."

"Is that world-shaking?"

"The Belgians, Claude told me, rub whipped cream in their hair. My beige man asked Gottlieb for whipped cream in his coffee."

"So your beige man is Armstrong? Pretty thin link, Bryce. All the same, we'll try to get a photo of Armstrong and run him down if he is in the city."

"Good. What I'm really interested in right now, Mr. Burgreen, is the fate of my wife."

Burgreen recalled that detail. "I shouldn't worry too much, if I were you. No signs of a struggle, were there?"

Henry couldn't say. No chairs or tables knocked over, nothing broken. "She could have been abducted by someone she knew."

"Let's not theorize. You just sit tight, and I'll call you back. If you hear from her—and I think you're going to—let me know at once."

Henry tried to settle down to wait. He tried to think what they could possibly have in the apartment that anyone would be so desperately anxious to find. He wondered how the searcher had managed to get in. Had Emily let him in? Usually she ignored the bell unless she knew who was ringing. There had been so many robberies in this part of town that it paid to be careful.

He looked through the binoculars at Geraldine's windows. The bamboo blinds were down tight, and a glow of light showed behind them.

He turned toward the windows in Quentin Hill's vacant apartment. Quite dark. Nothing going on there.

The liquor had got thin in his blood and he began to feel hungry. He could have one of poor Claude's steaks. He opened the freezing compartment, saw that Emily had stuffed the paper bag in there. She never could be taught that paper was an insulator. First you would have to explain what an insulator was.

The phone rang.

"Mr. Bryce? Cloche here. You are not engaged?"

"I'm waiting for a call about my wife," Henry said, and added silently, "Get off the phone, damn you."

"Your wife is not ill?"

"She's disappeared. Mr. Burgreen is looking for her."

"It is Mr. Burgreen I wished to ask you about. Do you know where I could reach him?"

"If it's important, I have his home phone."

"I don't know that it's important. But it is a curious fact."

Henry decided the quickest way to get him off the line was to give him Burgreen's phone number. He did so, Cloche thanked him, expressed his earnest desire for Mrs. Bryce's safe return, and hung up.

And maybe he knows exactly where she is, Henry thought. The letters in May's Beauty Salon seemed to him to implicate Monsieur Cloche more than anyone else in this thing, except of course the beige man.

Henry felt only mild curiosity about what Cloche wanted to tell Burgreen. He was thinking now about Emily's mother out on the Island, in Babylon. If something had happened to Emily, he would have to tell Mrs. Murdock. He was very much attached to Mrs. Murdock, and he dreaded the prospect. She would at this moment be sitting at her marbleized dining table under the bird cage chandelier which she only tolerated to please Emily, playing pinochle with the Morgans and Mrs. Bitney. Well, he would put off telling her as long as he decently could. Tomorrow morning at the earliest.

Again he went to the freezer, started to take out the steaks, and again the phone rang. Marie this time.

"Is Emily back yet? Henry, aren't you going to do anything?"

"I've called her friends. The police know. What else would you suggest?"

"Go out and look for her."

Louis said something to Marie, and Henry had to hold the phone away from his ear when she shouted, "Maybe it doesn't mean anything to you men that Emily is missing, but I'm not going to sit by and do nothing!" She slammed down the phone.

Henry gave up the idea of a steak, dropped a couple of eggs in a skillet, two pieces of Mrs. Bundy's No-Food-Value bread into the toaster, made a cup of instant, and presently sat down in the living room with this provender on a TV tray. He hadn't put back the stuff from the drawers and closets, not because he thought the police would want to see it as it was—the regular squad had no interest in a non-robbery, and Burgreen had said nothing about coming over—but only because he hadn't felt like doing it. He was still rocky from the blow he had received in May's, and the nap in the snow hadn't done him much good either.

He sat with his back to the windows in one of the white chairs with the cold rattling cellophane on it—Emily had these fits of covering everything with cellophane, and it was a most annoying habit, but just now he would have been deliriously happy to see her putting cellophane over the whole damned place. Funny how a person with Emily's abandoned attitude toward money should have these little hidden pockets of economy. She loved to mend. She would mend the most hopeless garment with the avidity of a squirrel. She patched sheets so that they rubbed pieces of hide off the innocent while they slept.

He finished his coffee, carried the tray to the kitchen, glanced at the red clock on the wall. After ten. The small knot of fear in his stomach grew tighter.

The phone again. He went toward it, telling himself it probably wasn't Emily. It wasn't.

"Is she back?" Burgreen demanded.

"No. Haven't you been looking?"

"Of course we've been looking. We checked the hospitals—"

"And the morgues?"

"Naturally. But if someone is holding her, there's not much chance of finding her in a hurry. We'll have to wait until they decide to make a move."

Henry wanted to know what kind of move Burgreen had in mind.

"A deal of some kind, maybe. It's evident they think you have something critical to their situation. If they took Emily with them they want to trade her for that critical something."

Henry said he couldn't imagine what it was they wanted. "We haven't brought home anything but food in the last few days. Certainly nothing from the Cloche apartment, or Geraldine's—or Bernard's."

That reminded Burgreen of the call from Monsieur Cloche. "He wanted to tell me he recognized Claude Bernard from a news photo he saw this afternoon."

"So?"

"Cloche says Bernard passed him and spoke to him on Park Avenue at about the time Mrs. Lorenz was departing for the next world."

"I can't see the importance of that."

Burgreen said something unflattering about Henry's intelligence. "If Bernard saw Cloche at that time, he knew that Cloche did not kill Mrs. Lorenz. Suppose he tried to sell that knowledge, or rather his silence, to the person who did kill her?"

"And stepped on a mine," Henry concluded. "Then Bernard must have known who did kill Camilla."

"I should think so," Burgreen agreed. "We don't know how he knew. But you said a friend of yours thought he had some scheme to help his bank account."

"It was more definite than that—it was a scheme to recover the money Armstrong owed him."

"Armstrong again."

Henry wondered how Cloche happened to speak to Bernard on Park Avenue at that particular moment, if he didn't know him.

"It was Bernard who spoke to Cloche. Harry Truman had just gone by, and Bernard asked Cloche who it was surrounded by reporters. Then Bernard recognized Cloche and wanted to re-hash all that painful stuff about the apartment, and Cloche was annoyed at a complete stranger accosting him in this way. I suppose that's why he remembered the face and recognized Bernard's picture in the newspaper."

"Too bad for Cloche that he's dead."

"On the other hand," Burgreen said slowly, "it might be very good for Cloche that he's dead. If Cloche is lying about this meeting on Park Avenue, no one can prove that he is, and it would be a clever and plausible alibi."

"He didn't strike me as that kind of man."

"Who knows what kind of man he is? You don't know him, Bryce. Neither do I. And I haven't found anyone else who does. He has friends at the UN, lots of them, but he doesn't confide in people. They all want to help him and they say it's so difficult because he keeps things to himself."

"Any diplomat has to learn that." Henry paused. "Doesn't this definitely bring Geraldine close to Bernard's murder? He was in her apartment, with my beige man, last night. It doesn't seem likely he was just socializing when he had such important matters on his mind as extortion."

"Possibly." Burgreen sounded dubious. "We've got a man watching Geraldine's apartment, but so far her friends and connections have been too cagey to call. I wonder how Bernard got onto her—if he did?"

Henry said he didn't know and neither did he care at this moment. All he cared about was the fate of Emily.

"We're doing everything we can, Bryce, I assure you." Burgreen threw him a few more words of encouragement and hung up.

Although he had been waiting for Burgreen to get off the phone so that Emily could call in—if she were able to call in—he now found the silence and emptiness of the rooms oppressive. He made another cup of coffee, wadded up the empty cigarette package, opened another, sat there smoking and staring at the red flannel Santa Claus. Gradually the lights went out in the windows around the block, except in Geraldine's. The refrigerator hummed for a few minutes, stopped. The heat had gone off long ago, and the apartment was cold.

The phone bell sounded like a fire engine. He sprang to it, full of hope.

"Oh, hello," he said dully. It was Marie again.

"Well, all I can say is, if she were alive, she'd have called you by now, Henry. She knows you're worried."

"She may be unable to get to a phone. If they're holding her somewhere."

Marie's bark was full of contempt for his innocence, his trust. "You and Louis. You just don't know the kind of people that live in this town. They don't hold you for ransom, they kill you and collect the ransom anyway and fly to Mexico."

Her scorn of the police was even greater than her scorn for Henry and Louis. "They only find you after your throat is cut. What do we pay them for? Look at the taxes on my building, I pay this city hundreds of dollars every year and the first time I want a little service what do I get? My best friend is in the hands of a killer and they can't even find her. I ask you! When I have a little extra garbage and I put it out in a carton because I can't get it in the can, I hear from them soon enough. They're right on the spot—very brave men when it comes to persecuting a poor woman and her coffee grounds. But looking for a murderer? Ha!"

Marie said she couldn't stay up any longer worrying about poor Emily, it was too late now to worry anyway, good night.

Henry's mind wandered over the people and events of the last few days, but he was too weary to do any constructive thinking. Bernard kept popping up, and he wondered if Monsieur Cloche were telling the truth about that walk on Park Avenue. If he were lying, then Cloche himself was pretty sure to be tied into the murder, as Burgreen suggested.

Henry recalled Claude Bernard's apparel on the day Mrs. Lorenz was murdered, in particular one item of that apparel. He looked at his watch. After twelve. Far too late to disturb anyone. He got up and went to the windows, saw that Geraldine had not yet gone to bed, but everybody else had. He paced to and fro, debating.

"To hell with his dignity," he said, and picked up the phone.

A voice came on almost immediately, "Cloche here."

Henry apologized for the hour, said he was sorry he hadn't been more interested when Monsieur Cloche called him about the encounter on Park Avenue, and expressed great interest in it.

"It did seem significant to me," Cloche admitted, "and I believe Mr. Burgreen found it so, although he is not given to great enthusiasm."

"No, he isn't. A point has occurred to me—do you happen to recall the necktie Claude Bernard was wearing when you met him?"

"Of course. I told Mr. Burgreen. He had a most repulsive mauve affair, obviously real silk, embroidered with a large watch, the hands of which were gems—not real, of course."

"Eureka!" Henry said.

"Pardon?"

"That's the right answer, man."

"Thank you," Cloche said dryly. "I gather you thought I might be lying."

"It's all in the business, nothing personal."

Cloche asked about Emily, and expressed sorrow at the news, and was about to hang up when Henry detained him. So long as Cloche was under suspicion it hadn't been wise to ask him, but now it was surely all right.

"Do you know anything about the Royal Development Company of Celestia?"

"Yes," Cloche said. "It's a company set up by some Americans to speculate in land, especially around Celestia where growth is rapid. I believe they also have some mining properties."

"You don't know who they are, these Americans?"

Cloche paused. "I did know the name of one of them—Francine met him at a party at home, and it seems to me we entertained him. I'll ask her when she wakes."

Henry asked if the Royal Development Company could have a grievance against Pierre Cloche.

"Not against me, but possibly against the government I represent." Cloche explained that such companies feared expropriation. His administration had rather ambitious plans for land reform, and these would bring disappointment to those who wished to gain through speculation. "We would pay for the land, of course, but not the prices such speculators would anticipate in a free market. Celestia is growing fantastically, not only through migration from the interior, but as a tourist center—cruise ships find it attractive, and with the landing of more and more tourists the space for shops has been in great demand, and prices naturally rise."

"In other words a collision here between private interests and government plans?" Henry summed up.

Cloche agreed. "There have always been powerful groups who opposed us, people who saw an opportunity to make a fortune out of the country's new growth."

Henry wished Cloche would wake up his wife to ask her the name of the man from the Royal Development Company whom she had entertained in Celestia, but he didn't like to suggest it.

Cloche sneezed. He was probably standing there in his night-shirt. Henry let him go, and went back to the windows. There was still a light in Geraldine's apartment. He looked down on the maze of yards and fences, and suddenly stiffened. There was someone down there, a moving shadow among shadows. Henry groped for the glasses without taking his eyes off the figure, focused, saw a woman in a fur coat. She moved toward the Lexington Avenue side, reached a fence in the middle of the block, threw something over it, and then with some difficulty climbed the fence herself. He lost her as she dropped over.

There seemed no answer to this incident, so he sat down again and returned to the matter of Claude Bernard.

That silly straw hat. He could see Emily in it now, admiring herself in the rococo gilt mirror. She carried it off very well—Emily could wear anything, the more extreme the better.

What the devil had Claude Bernard been doing with that hat? He wasn't going to a masquerade, was he? Burgreen hadn't mentioned finding anything else that went with the hat. There would have been a dress, petticoats, gloves, shoes—No, no masquerade. Something had been ripped off the hat, obviously.

Feathers? Ribbon? Flowers?

Feathers. A plume. And a gold turban! He went to the window again and looked across at the dark panes on the third floor of Quentin Hill's building. Claude had been watching from that apartment, dressed up like nothing on this earth because he knew that Emily used her binoculars on everything in the block, and he didn't want to be recognized. Who was he watching? Geraldine? Undoubtedly Geraldine, because it was in Geraldine's apartment that he had met the beige man.

Henry went to the phone to call Burgreen, hesitated. The poor guy was probably getting his best sleep right now. But a severe grilling of Geraldine Seabrook seemed to be indicated. If she was in the middle of it, she could tell them where Emily was— or at least who might have abducted her.

Henry dialed the Staten Island number.

The deep voice became slowly enraged. "What the hell does it matter that he wore a Floradora plume and a sheet while he watched your friend Geraldine?" Burgreen snarled. "We knew he was in her apartment. We knew he was later murdered. This is only a minor detail, Bryce. Now will you for God's sake get off this phone and let me sleep?"

"It's a minor detail that shows he was intensely interested in that apartment and who went to it. It shows he wasn't just there for a friendly cocktail last night before he was murdered," Henry insisted.

"I wish you wouldn't try to use your brain. Terrible things happen to men who strain their mental powers." Burgreen broke the connection.

As soon as Henry put down the phone, it rang.

ELEVEN

"Is she back?" Link demanded.

"No. Where have you been?"

"I told you I had a date with this barn woman from Jersey. It worked out according to plan, the only problem now is to get the cannon across the river to the barn. But never mind about that—I was sure Emily would come back safe and sound, with some logical explanation like a knitting lesson at Carnegie Hall or something. You must be in a sweat. I'll come over."

"No, don't. There's nothing you can do." He told Link about his theory that Claude Bernard had been watching Geraldine and had found out who killed Mrs. Lorenz. "I just got hell from Burgreen because I wanted him to grill Geraldine and find out if she knows anything about Emily. He seems to want to do nothing but sleep at night."

But Burgreen was not sleeping. In a few minutes the phone whirred again.

"Your friend Geraldine is gone," the detective announced with some sourness. "I had a good man watching her, never thought he'd let her get away. He swears he didn't go to sleep or leave his post. He could see the entrance to her building. He's never slept on a job before."

"She didn't go out the front door, maybe," Henry suggested.

Burgreen wanted to know how she could leave the building by any other door.

"I'll tell you how she left and what she was wearing. She went down the fire escape and crossed the block through the yards to Lexington. She was wearing a fur coat and carrying a suitcase."

"If you saw her, for God's sake why didn't you let me know?"

"I didn't know it was Geraldine—maybe it wasn't, but I saw a woman doing that a while ago, while I was sitting here wondering about Emily. Any word on my wife?"

"No. How could this Geraldine get over the fence, and even if she got over the fence, how could she get out onto Lexington Avenue? She'd have to go through a building."

That, Henry said, would probably come to light. "Better check the airports."

"Yes, Mother." Burgreen was really sour now.

"And it just occurred to me that May's place on Thirty-eighth is pretty handy to the East Side Terminal and all those public lockers. Maybe the correspondence has been put there till somebody can get it out of the country. Geraldine, for instance." Henry was pleased with this thought, and he went on to tell Burgreen how he had proved the innocence of Monsieur Cloche by a necktie.

Burgreen made a disrespectful noise. "How do you know when Cloche saw Bernard's mauve silk necktie? He could have seen it any time on Wednesday."

Henry sadly agreed that this was so.

Sometime after that, in spite of his resolve, he fell asleep with his feet on the coffee table.

At seven o'clock Marie phoned, and he couldn't sleep after that. He had some foul coffee, and was shivering in the cold kitchen when Link called.

"No word from Burgreen?" he asked anxiously.

"No. Nothing."

Link tried to find words of comfort, but they were so obviously forced that they only served to underline the stark possibilities in Emily's disappearance.

Henry ate a soggy English muffin, put on a clean shirt and went out to get the Sunday papers.

It had been snowing all night, and it was still snowing. The avenue was quilted. Even a lonely bus, puffing evil gases, snarled in a muffled way. There was no one in sight, all sensible souls were staying inside. Henry had no taste for Sunday in New York anyway—there was always a barren aimlessness about it, and it depressed him to think of the unshaven husbands slumped under a mass of rumpled newspaper, smelling like the dregs of Saturday night. Only Chinatown was alert, washed and dressed, and about its business of selling exhumed duck. He didn't feel he could journey to Chinatown for cheer this morning.

He picked up the papers from inside the drugstore—no papers outside today—and hurried home. All the time he was out he was rasped by the thought that Emily or her captors might be trying to reach him on the phone. The elevator seemed to rise with unusual sluggishness.

The phone was ringing as he unlocked the door, and he had a rush of hope as he sprinted to it. Burgreen. Henry sagged.

"Dead end everywhere," Burgreen reported, after Henry told him Emily was not there. "All planes grounded. No flights out of either airport since you thought you saw Miss Seabrook climbing fences. No person definitely answering her description purchased a plane ticket from any of the terminals in town, and she's not waiting around at La Guardia or Idlewild. May show up, of course, as soon as flights resume. We've got men posted. Got a photograph from her apartment, and that helps. The human physiognomy is not easily described with accuracy."

"How do you know she isn't hiding in a ladies' room?"

"Women checked. Also checked lockers in East Side Terminal. No soap." A more brilliant idea struck Henry. Perhaps the files were now in the Cloche apartment.

"We thought of that," Burgreen told him. "We'll have to do a lot of bowing and scraping to gain our objective—no right to search his place, you know."

In the middle of this conversation the buzzer sounded, and Henry found Fred Wheeler at the door, apologetic for the early hour. "I came into town to do some work on my wife's affairs, and phoned Mrs. Cloche to ask her about some details on that job. She told me your wife is missing. I had to come over, Bryce. This is terrible."

"It is," Henry agreed. "Come in. I'm on the phone." He returned to Burgreen. "Have you done anything about fingerprints in the back room at Thirty-eighth Street? I took the makeup bottle from there. Might have good prints on it."

"We're ahead of you. Not a known criminal."

"Who thought it was? A known criminal sleeping in blue percale—"

"That's not so impossible. But we have another angle on your blue percale friend. Let you know about that later, if it jells."

"I wish to God you'd do something about Emily."

"What do you think we are doing? Until we nail down one of the principals, we don't have any way of locating Mrs. Bryce. That is, if she's been detained by them."

"What do you mean, if? She's been out all night. Emily likes a comfortable bed." Henry was particularly bitter because he remembered he had to tell Mrs. Murdock about Emily before too many hours went by, and he dreaded the job.

When he put down the phone, Wheeler wanted to know all about it. Henry gave him a brief summary. "Who is Geraldine?" he interrupted once. Henry pointed out her windows across the block. Wheeler gave a surprised whistle, entertained himself with the binoculars. It looked as if he were going to spend the day, poor guy. He was an awful color, must have been awake for several nights. It was hard to imagine anyone's mourning deeply over Camilla, but evidently Fred was shaken by her death.

"I can't see any possible connection between my wife and

this fellow Armstrong," he said. "I doubt if they even knew each other."

"Camilla sent Armstrong to Bernard when she found out Armstrong's credit was no good."

"How did she find that out?"

"August Boomer ... The only reason I can see for your wife's death is that it would completely finish Pierre Cloche."

"How?" Wheeler asked. He seemed pretty slow on the up-take this morning.

"Cloche was the natural suspect—furious with Mrs. Lorenz for her job on his apartment, and the newspaper stories."

Wheeler nodded vaguely, and Henry went on. "But Claude Bernard knew Cloche did not kill your wife—Claude saw Cloche on Park Avenue at the time Camilla was being murdered."

"Is that so?"

"We figure Claude tried to blackmail the real murderer, and got himself killed. If Armstrong is the man in the camel's hair coat, and I think he is, then he and Geraldine probably killed both your wife and Claude Bernard."

Wheeler sighed, sank into one of the white armchairs.

"Get up a minute and I'll take off that cellophane," Henry offered. "My wife's idea. Drives me mad."

"Your poor wife," Fred murmured, and the words, sad and sympathetic, sent a chill through Henry, as if Emily were already dead.

Marie called again. Would Henry come over there? They hated to think of him all alone in his apartment, worrying and wait-ing. Louis thought he should come for dinner. She thought so too. She was making a dish he liked—veal stuffed with spinach and egg.

"I'm not alone," Henry explained. "Fred Wheeler is here keep-ing me company. We've got some steaks. I think I'll stay here, just in case." Louis came on, tried to persuade him, but Henry was firm.

He thought he'd better thaw the steaks and went to the refrigerator. Fred followed him like a sad dog.

Henry opened the freezing compartment, took out the large paper bag. It seemed very full. He untwisted the top and looked in. Brown tweed. He dumped the bag on the kitchen table. The steaks and broccoli were there, at the bottom, under a pair of very good tweed slacks.

"You always keep your pants on ice?" Wheeler asked.

"Now where do you suppose she picked those up? She took the steaks from poor old Claude and we went on from his apartment to Geraldine's, and then we came back here—that is, I think she came straight in. I left her in the street. So the chances are she collected these slacks in Geraldine's. It's a wonder Burgreen didn't see her." Henry looked at the label in the band—*J. Rossi, Custom Tailor*.

The phone rang, and Henry dashed for it. Link again.

"No word from Emily. Fred Wheeler's here." He glanced behind him at Wheeler, who had settled on the couch and was lighting a cigarette. "We just made a discovery. Emily snatched a pair of tweed slacks from somewhere—probably Geraldine's apartment. If so she got them out under the eyes of Burgreen in a brown paper sack."

"So your girl friend had a boyfriend. What size are these slacks?" Link asked.

"Wait till I look." Henry fetched them from the kitchen. "I'd say a forty. Tailor's label in the band—J. Rossi."

"Rossi has a shop on Madison—not large, but plush. He'd know who he made the pants for."

Henry went on speculating. "Those empty hangers in Geraldine's closets probably held his clothes, not hers. She got rid of them, but overlooked the tweed slacks."

"But why was she getting rid of her boyfriend's clothes?" Link wondered.

"She was getting rid of him—or he was leaving voluntarily. I wonder what she did with the stuff that must have been in that file?"

Link pointed out that he didn't know whether anything had been in the file. Henry didn't think people cluttered up an apartment with filing cases for no purpose. "She was carrying on some kind of business there," he insisted, "and she got rid of the records, whatever they were."

"Now the big question is, who was her boyfriend and business partner. Would the slacks fit your man in the camel's hair coat?"

Henry was sure they were too large. He picked them up again, held them against himself, and as he did so, something rolled across the coffee table and fell into the carpet. "Hold on," he said and put down the phone, began to search in the deep soft pile of the rug.

Wheeler leaned forward. "What are you looking for?"

"Something fell out of the slacks." Henry's fingers found a small, smooth bead. He held it in his palm for Wheeler to see, took the phone again. "Pearl. Looks like a good one."

"Geraldine's, maybe?" Link suggested.

"Maybe." Henry recalled a scene, unpleasant and vivid—Miss Ash and Julian Pointer accusing each other in connection with the missing pearl from Camilla's necklace.

"Is it a real pearl?" Link asked.

"I'm no pearl expert. Maybe Wheeler knows." Henry had his back to Wheeler, and he turned now to smile at him. The smile slid away. There was a change in Wheeler. He was no longer sitting back easily on the couch, smoking. He sat hunched forward, watching Henry, his eyes intent, unblinking.

Link's voice came through the phone loud and clear—too loud and clear. "You said Camilla was wearing a pearl necklace, and it broke when she was strangled. Suppose one of her pearls dropped into the cuff of these slacks—"

Wheeler was listening. He seemed scarcely to breathe.

"Marie just called," Henry told Link, hoping to steer him away from the pearls. "She says—"

"My God, Henry, whoever wore those pants strangled Camilla!"

He had to cut Link off. In a voice that he felt must be a quivering falsetto, he said, "Marie says you don't use cheese in that kind of *paste*." He hung up.

"Was that Simpson?" Wheeler asked casually. "I suppose he's anxious about Mrs. Bryce, too."

"Yes. Quite concerned." Henry looked around the room, saw the box of tree ornaments. Glass balls, gossamer snow and tinsel, cardboard angels and stars, brittle candy canes and jolly mistletoe. It was regrettable that everything to do with the Christmas spirit was so light and airy, so ineffectual in a situation calling for a crowbar. In the apartment above theirs Gregory Hammacher was up. Henry could hear his big feet clumping around, and then the first waves of hi-fi disturbance. Gregory could help, if only he knew. There was no way to let him know. Down the hall lived an ill-tempered bulldog. There was no way to let him know either. The pale light of Sunday fell gently on the white carpet, and the room was quiet.

Wheeler looked at his watch. "You know, Bryce, I think if you'll forgive me, I'll change my mind about the steak. Awfully kind of you, and I appreciate it, but I believe I'll go home." He stood up.

Henry waited.

The pearl lay in a green enamel ash tray on the table beside the tweed slacks. Suddenly Wheeler leaned over, seized the pearl and the trousers, shot across the room toward the door. Henry leaped after him, grabbed him as he opened the door, but Wheeler kept on going, dragging Henry with him into the hall. Then with a heavy blow he caught Henry under the jaw, jerking his head back against the wall.

Henry buckled, slid, his skull struck the concrete floor. He was sure his brains were oozing onto the tile, but he was conscious, he could still see.

Wheeler reached the elevator and pressed the button, looked round at Henry, saw that he was prone, completely ineffectual. Wheeler, once in the elevator, was gone—on his way out of the country. Henry tried to make his legs move tried to raise himself with his arms. Nothing functioned. He was as limp as an oyster.

The elevator was coming now—Wheeler stepped forward expectantly, prepared to glide through the door as soon as it opened.

The door opened. Wheeler moved gladly toward it. And stopped.

The elevator door was wide enough to allow the passage of a man and a fox terrier, but not a man and a boxer. Coming through it now was an improbable object, very wide and about five and a half feet tall. A Christmas tree. Behind the tree, holding it by the trunk, came Emily. She was also carrying a very large potted poinsettia. That no one could work his way into the elevator while she was working hers out was immediately apparent to Henry, but not to Wheeler. Wheeler tried to get past her.

Emily's next move was one of pure courtesy and kindness. She had no grasp of the situation, but saw that Mr. Wheeler was trying to get in. To make way for him she raised the potted plant above her head, juggled in a frenzied effort to balance it, lost control, and as he ducked, dropped the thing on the back of his neck. Wheeler staggered, crumpled, and lay full length.

Emily stood looking down at him, surprised and apologetic, still holding the Christmas tree by its trunk like a mace. "I'm terribly sorry, Mr. Wheeler," she said. "I didn't mean to hurt you."

Wheeler wasn't out, and he started to move. Henry cried, "Hit him again!" but Emily, for the first time seeing Henry on the floor, was confused.

"Hit him again," Henry cried.

Emily dropped the tree and ran to him. "What's the matter, Henry? Why are you lying on the floor?"

Wheeler stirred, sat up.

Henry, gritting his teeth against the pain in his head, struggled to his feet and stood over Wheeler. "Stay where you are," he ordered in something less than a commanding voice.

Wheeler smiled. He was going to get up, and Henry knew he couldn't stop him. The elevator was still there, and Wheeler would get into it this time.

There was a sudden clatter of shoe leather and voices, and Link and Burgreen, with two police officers, came panting from the stairway.

"Good work, Bryce," Burgreen said, looking down at Wheeler. He nodded to one of the officers, who fastened bracelets on the man.

"Don't think I had anything to do with it," Henry said. "Emily knocked him out."

"I didn't mean to hit him," Emily explained, bewildered. "I had the Christmas tree and my handbag and the plant, and things got a little unbalanced."

"You all right, Henry?" Link gave him a worried inspection.

"My head has a slight fissure in it. Otherwise sound."

"Could we have a little session in your place, Bryce?" Burgreen suggested.

TWELVE

"Henry, what happened to our apartment?" Emily cried, looking around at the disorder.

"Never mind that. Where have you been?"

"Didn't you get my note? I left a note right on the coffee table." She turned to Wheeler. "I suppose he took it, if he's the one."

"He is the one. And where were you?"

"At Mama's, in Babylon. Somebody called me while Mr. Wheeler was here, and said Mama needed me right away. An emergency. She didn't want me at all. She didn't call me, Henry. I suppose it was one of his co-workers." Again she looked at Wheeler.

"But why didn't you let me know?" Henry demanded.

"I was afraid you'd worry. You know these fake phone calls always come before they kidnap a person, or kill them. So I knew I'd have to stay all night or they'd grab me at the Long Island station. Mama was glad to have me. She had a good dinner—chicken pie and lemon tarts. One lemon tart—she didn't expect me."

Burgreen held up a hand. "If we try to trace the workings of Mrs. Bryce's mind, we'll never get to the bottom of this. We picked up Miss Seabrook at Idlewild with a suitcase full of correspondence for the Royal Development Company. With her was Hazen Armstrong—your beige man in the camel's hair coat, Bryce."

"Henry was right all the time—there was a beige man," Link said with some surprise.

Henry's satisfaction was diluted with pain. His head throbbed. "How did you know I was in trouble?" he asked them.

"I called the precinct," Link explained. "I knew by the way you talked somebody was with you, and you were, shall we say, a little nervous?"

"Let's say scared green."

"The precinct sent a couple of men and also relayed the message to me as I came in from Idlewild," Burgreen added. "Naturally I didn't linger to finish my crocheting. Where do you figure in this, Wheeler?"

"Geraldine was his girlfriend," Henry said.

Wheeler had gone back to his sad, innocent, hound-dog look. "I don't even know this Geraldine."

"Then why were you so anxious to get hold of the trousers Emily took from Geraldine's apartment?" Henry asked.

"Oh, is that whose they are?" Emily looked at the trousers with great interest. "I thought when I saw them in that hamper in Geraldine's bathroom they might be something we could use—in the case, I mean."

Wheeler still maintained they were not his—he recognized them as belonging to a friend, and only wanted to save the friend embarrassment.

"The friend was yourself," Henry insisted. "Those empty hangers in Geraldine's apartment had held your clothes. You removed everything else, but overlooked these trousers, and discovered later that you didn't have them. Geraldine remembered they were in the hamper, and since we had been in her apartment, concluded we had taken them. So one of you searched here for them."

"Mr. Wheeler was here when I got the call to go out to Mama's," Emily said. "A woman made the call."

"Geraldine," Link guessed.

"And while Wheeler was here he managed to get your key," Henry said to Emily, "so he could come back and look for the trousers."

"That's where my key is—I was looking for it on the way in." Emily turned to Wheeler indignantly. "Why did you have to send me clear out to Babylon on a cold clammy local? You know what those afternoon trains are. That wasn't very nice."

"He wanted time," Henry told her. "He figured I was good for a couple of hours over at the St. Regis, getting a haircut—I assume you told him I was going to the St. Regis?"

Emily nodded. Burgreen, meanwhile, had been looking at the tweed trousers. He addressed Wheeler. "I'm sure Mr. Rossi can tell us who he made these for."

Wheeler slid down in his chair. "After all, it's no crime to leave an article of clothing in a lady's apartment, is it? I didn't want Miss Seabrook to be dragged into this."

"I'm afraid Miss Seabrook has been in it from the beginning, with both feet," Burgreen said, and turned to one of the officers. "Go down and tell McNulty to bring up Armstrong and the lady."

"They're downstairs?" Emily cried.

"I didn't take time to drop them at the precinct. When I got the message, I came."

"Has anybody a few words of one syllable they could spare me? How did it begin? Who did what?"

"It began, I think, with the Royal Development Company of Celestia, Gaad," Burgreen told her. "Wheeler could simplify things by telling us about that, but I don't suppose he will."

Wheeler gave him a bitter look. "I had nothing to do with it. I was simply attached, very foolishly it seems, to Miss Seabrook."

Burgreen took out his pipe and his Galvin's Mixture. "The company bought large tracts of land around Celestia, later to be sold off in small parcels at a good profit. Perhaps they had mining properties too. The present administration of the government of Gaad opposed such schemes. Problem: How to discredit the administration, cause it to fall?"

"It's all news to me," Wheeler maintained.

The door opened and McNulty brought in Hazen Armstrong and Miss Seabrook. Henry recognized the man in the camel's hair coat, even though Armstrong had removed the beige makeup and revealed a fresh complexion with color in the cheeks and the overnight growth of a dark beard. He had the grieved pouting look of a spoiled child.

"I admire your accomplishments," Henry told him. "You're as good with a paint brush as you are with a gat."

He glared. "Your opinions don't interest me, Mr. Bryce."

Emily studied him. "I hope you've brought your razor. Mr. Armstrong. You'll need a shave before dinner, and they're very particular in the Tombs."

Geraldine was still wearing the mink coat, but her hair was stringy and she had eaten off her lipstick. "Fred, I told you not to risk coming here again for those silly trousers," she scolded.

"I couldn't risk letting Bryce find them. They were an easy link to you and Armstrong. There was nothing else to implicate me in the Cloche affair."

"Once we were all out of the country, it would have made no difference."

"I didn't want to leave the country." Wheeler scowled.

"You won't have to now," Burgreen assured him. "Miss Seabrook, how did you manage to get out onto Lexington Avenue last night?"

"Through the French bakery. It's open all night."

"And perhaps you'll tell us something about the Royal Development Company. Wheeler says he never heard of it."

"Now Fred, there's no sense in being obstinate," she told him. "The company was formed by Mr. Armstrong and Mr. Wheeler to develop the resources of Gaad. A sound and worthy enterprise," she added. "Those natives don't know how to use what they have, and they were being misled by the dreadful Cloche family—threats of expropriation, laws about foreigners and that sort of thing. We were only planning to help rid the country of undesirable elements. Isn't that so, Hazen?"

Armstrong looked at his shoes, said nothing.

"Who put up the money?" Burgreen demanded.

"Both of them," Geraldine answered. "Hazen had a nice inheritance, and he put it all into this venture, which left him rather strapped and led to the embarrassing thing about his bill with Claude Bernard. Fred put almost everything he had into the company, too, didn't you, Fred?"

"So if the scheme didn't work, they would both be broke. It had to work. You planned to discredit the government of Gaad so it would fall, and a more friendly regime be installed. You wanted to make Cloche look extravagant and frivolous, so there would be an outcry here about a U.S. loan to such a government. If the loan fell through, the administration would probably collapse."

"In brief, yes. Mrs. Cloche was very gullible. That made it easy to persuade her the decorating was a gift."

Henry turned to Armstrong. "Why the makeup? And why did you move to that awful hole on Thirty-eighth?"

Armstrong opened his mouth to answer, but Geraldine cut him off. "Hazen was known to members of the Gaad delegation, including Pierre Cloche. He had been in Gaad. It began with a mine he inherited from his mother. He went to Gaad to see about the mine, and got excited about the country. He and Fred set up the Royal Development Company. Hazen couldn't risk being recognized while he engineered the publicity stunt with the Cloche apartment. He had to be officially out of town. You forced him out of the Boulogne, Mr. Bryce, when you followed him there. Then Hazen rented the building on Thirty-eighth, and we moved the correspondence to that location."

Henry wanted to know why they had thought it necessary to use the portraits of Marx and Engels on the secretary. Wheeler said he was opposed to that. "I thought they were overdoing it, but Geraldine thought it added fuel to the fire. A Marxist wouldn't be buying gold pianos and satin walls."

"They're like other people in their love of luxury," Geraldine argued. "The papers seemed to swallow both ideas."

Burgreen cut off this tangent. "Did Mrs. Lorenz know the real reason for decorating the Cloche apartment?"

"No," Wheeler told him, "she had nothing to do with the company."

"Why did you kill her?"

Geraldine whirled on him. "Fred did not kill his wife! Pierre Cloche strangled Camilla in a fit of rage over what she had done to his career."

"We have reason to believe Cloche was somewhere else at the time. You didn't go to Washington at all, did you, Wheeler? You suddenly saw an excellent opportunity to get rid of your wife and have someone else blamed. Or was Camilla's murder part of the plan from the beginning—just to make sure Cloche was completely blackened?"

"It was not part of the plan, and Fred didn't do it," Geraldine cried.

Burgreen plodded on. "Wheeler knew that Julian Pointer went out to lunch at twelve, and came back when he got ready. Miss Ash went out at twelve-thirty and came back in half an hour, so as not to keep Mrs. Lorenz waiting. Half an hour alone with your wife was plenty of time, wasn't it, Wheeler?"

"Don't answer, Fred," Geraldine ordered. "He has no proof, he's just fishing. You don't have to say a word."

Burgreen didn't look particularly pleased with Miss Seabrook. "If it upsets you to remember your wife's murder, Wheeler, per-haps we could discuss the butcher knife and Claude Bernard. Was that necessary?" Wheeler was silent. "Bernard, we know now, was watching Miss Seabrook's apartment. How long he had been doing so, we don't know. But he saw you there, and assumed the connection between you and Miss Seabrook. He already knew that Cloche was walking on Park Avenue at the time Mrs. Lorenz was strangled, so he looked for another suspect. Who is more logical than a husband in such cases? A husband who chafes under a tight rein, who would be able to use his wife's money, and who in addition has a girlfriend? Bernard confronted you with his conclusions, and asked for money. He was seen in Miss Seabrook's apartment on Friday night, along with Armstrong. Some trap must have been quickly arranged. Perhaps you asked Bernard to drive you to your office to get the cash? You availed yourself of the handiest weapon you could find in a hurry—a butcher knife from Miss Seabrook's kitchen. When Bernard parked his car near your office building you knifed him, drove the Mercedes back to Sixty-second Street and parked it, leaving the body in the car."

Geraldine snapped open her cigarette lighter. Her hand shook only a little. "A lovely case, Mr. Burgreen. If only you had some proof."

"There's the little matter of the pearl," Link said mildly.

"Pearl?" Burgreen repeated.

Henry explained. "The pearl that fell out of Wheeler's trousers when I took them from the refrigerator. We know that when Camilla was strangled her pearl necklace broke. One of the pearls was missing. It fell into the trouser cuff of the murderer."

Geraldine laughed. "Fantastic. That wouldn't happen in a hundred years."

"Where is the pearl?" Emily wanted to know.

"Wheeler has it," Henry said.

Burgreen found it on him, but Geraldine would not give up. "How do you know this is a pearl from Camilla's necklace?"

"We don't know, yet," Burgreen admitted. "We'll ask Tiffany to compare it with the others. But Wheeler has admitted he thinks it's one of her pearls by trying to run off with it."

Miss Seabrook turned on Fred. "You have no judgment!"

"Is that so? This whole thing is your fault."

"My fault!"

"If you weren't so damned systematic, and so goddamned bossy, you wouldn't have put my slacks in that cleaning hamper, in fact you wouldn't have a cleaning hamper. Nobody else has two hampers in the bathroom. If you'd left those slacks in the closet where I put them, I'd have taken them away with the other things and this never would have happened."

Burgreen wondered why Miss Seabrook thought the slacks should be cleaned. If he thought he could trap her into saying something about incriminating hairs or lint he was mistaken. She merely thought they needed a good pressing.

"Why didn't you take them to the cleaner at once?" he went on.

"Because I always take things to the cleaner on Monday."

Wheeler sighed. "You see."

Emily thought someone ought to call poor Monsieur Cloche, who was still in miserable ignorance. Burgreen said that would be done in good time. He turned his attention to Armstrong, asked if he had known about the murders. Armstrong stated that he knew nothing at all about them, his was purely a business arrangement to promote the company.

"Nice business," Burgreen muttered. "You took advantage of Cloche, who had never done you any harm, and set out to ruin him for a profit."

"A man has to live."

"Even if he exposes someone else to a charge of murder."

"That wasn't my doing, and anyway, Cloche would never be charged, you know that, Mr. Burgreen. Diplomatic immunity."

"A worse fate, probably, than being charged and tried—no opportunity to clear himself."

Link was puzzled. "Armstrong surely knew Wheeler had killed Claude Bernard? Cloche had no motive for that."

Armstrong was silent, and Henry suggested that Armstrong couldn't expose Wheeler without exposing himself and the Cloche plot. Wheeler was safe, as far as Armstrong was concerned.

The phone rang, and Henry lifted it. Quentin Hill began in a husky voice, "Bryce, I've been thinking about that business of the third-floor apartment. It could have been Claude Bernard up there."

"What makes you think so?" Henry asked innocently.

Hill cleared his throat, came out with the thing that had been gnawing his conscience. "I told Bernard about what went on in that Park Avenue apartment. I didn't know the woman, but I knew Fred Wheeler. He's a customer. Claude seemed interested. I just thought I ought to warn you, before something happened to you or Mrs. Bryce."

"The warning's a little late, but thanks anyway. Better tell the detective about this." Henry handed the phone to Burgreen.

After that Burgreen and his men took the members of the Royal Development Company away. McNulty came back in a moment with the Christmas tree. "I found this in the hall. You'll be wanting it. Merry Christmas!"

"I'm starved," Link announced. "Let's eat those steaks."

"I've spent enough time with those steaks," Henry protested. "Let's go out and get something less macabre."

Emily got into her new black dress and they went to the St. Regis, which had a peaceful Sunday evening feeling. Settled at the bar, they went over the strange behavior of Fred Wheeler.

"Why would he choose a girlfriend like Geraldine?" Emily asked. "She's as bossy and disagreeable as Camilla was."

Link took a long swallow of bourbon and looked at her gravely. "A man repeats his mistakes, Emily darling."

Henry agreed. "My next wife will be a slob."

"I'm cut to the core," Emily wailed. "Couldn't you say 'slightly disorderly?'"

"My next wife will be a slightly disorderly slob."

Emily smiled, raised her glass of fruit salad and vodka, and suddenly remembered Marie. "She still thinks I'm dead in a vacant lot! Poor Marie. Go call her, Henry."

"You call her."

Emily did. "I think Marie was a little disappointed," she said, coming back. "She had a dress in mind to wear to my funeral. But Louis was awfully relieved. He thinks you're heroic, Henry. Do you feel heroic?"

"Terribly. Nothing makes a man feel more heroic than lying on the floor while his wife captures a murderer with a poinsettia."

In a day or two, when the story got around, the Irish rejoiced that an English plot had been exposed, the Russians believed the American State Department had been undone, and Monsieur Cloche felt free once more to sleep through a meeting of the Committee on Outer Space.

THE END

If you enjoyed *The Diplomat and the Gold Piano,* ask your bookseller for Emily and Henry's first three cases, *The Gun in Daniel Webster's Bust* (0-915230-74-7, $14.95), *The Green Plaid Pants* (0-915230-80-1, $14.95) and *The Glass on the Stairs* (0-915230-90-9). The Rue Morgue intends to publish all four titles in this series as well as those featuring the Rev. Martin Buell plus several stand-alones. Details on The Rue Morgue may be found on the next page.

About the Rue Morgue Press

"Rue Morgue Press is the old-mystery lover's best friend, reprinting high quality books from the 1930s and '40s."
—*Ellery Queen's Mystery Magazine*

Since 1997, the Rue Morgue Press has reprinted scores of traditional mysteries, the kind of books that were the hallmark of the Golden Age of detective fiction. Authors reprinted or to be reprinted by the Rue Morgue include Catherine Aird, Dorothy Bowers, Pamela Branch, Joanna Cannan, Glyn Carr, Torrey Chanslor, Clyde B. Clason, Joan Coggin, Manning Coles, Lucy Cores, Frances Crane, Norbert Davis, Elizabeth Dean, Constance & Gwenyth Little, Marlys Millhiser, James Norman, Stuart Palmer, Craig Rice, Kelley Roos, Charlotte Murray Russell, Maureen Sarsfield, Margaret Scherf and Juanita Sheridan.

To suggest titles or to receive a catalog of Rue Morgue Press books write P.O. Box 4119, Boulder, CO 80306, telephone 800-699-6214, or check out our website, www.ruemorguepress.com, which lists complete descriptions of all of our titles, along with lengthy biographies of our writers.